ICE QUAKE

Coming soon, more adventures for Michael and Katya in:

Firestorm

A division of Hachette Children's Books

For Andrea and Matthew

First published in Great Britain in 2010
by Hodder Children's Books

1

A Catalogue record for this book is available from the British Library

ISBN-13: 978 0 340 99886 1

Typeset in AGaramond by Avon DataSet Ltd,
Bidford on Avon, Warwickshire

Printed and bound in Great Britain by
CPI Bookmarque Ltd, Croydon, Surrey

The paper and board used in this paperback by Hodder Children's Books are natural recyclable products made from wood grown in sustainable forests. The manufacturing processes conform to the environmental regulations of the country of origin.

Hodder Children's Books
a division of Hachette Children's Books
338 Euston Road, London NW1 3BH
An Hachette UK company
www.hachette.co.uk

Prologue: The Hunters

Baring Island, Northwest Territories, Canada
64°33′S 62°02′W

The hunter had paid fifty thousand dollars to kill a polar bear – and he wasn't going home without one.

They'd been out from Miller's Harbour for three frustrating days, without even the hint of a bear. But at last they had picked up the trail early that morning and were now preparing to move in for the kill.

Pretty soon the skin would be hanging on the wall of his den back in Milwaukee, and all his pals who went out shooting harmless creatures like rabbits or deer would be green with envy. They would know that he'd taken on the mightiest carnivore on God's earth and defeated it.

Usually he was an accountant. He lived in the

suburbs, he wore a boring grey suit, and the most exciting part of his day was getting on a train in the morning. He wasn't fabulously wealthy, but he was rich, and like many rich people he was very, very bored.

But not on this day.

If his friends could see him now, standing on the ice plain, the temperature minus thirty, all kitted out in his fur-trimmed parka, his face mask and tinted goggles, his binoculars hanging around his neck, the huskies barking around him, they would be jealous as hell – particularly when they saw him raise his rifle and scan the horizon. Not just any rifle, either. It was a .300 Winchester Magnum, the kind snipers used in the army, accurate to 1100 metres.

For this one day out of his whole life, John Gordon Liddy III was a man of action.

It would also be the day he died.

Liddy and his Inuit guide, Paul Nappaaluk, had been tracking the bear for about an hour. Liddy's excitement was visibly growing, but it was hard to tell with Paul. He was a small, weather-beaten man, and he didn't say much, didn't react to anything. Liddy could hardly even guess his age – maybe somewhere between sixty and seventy, perhaps even eighty. He wasn't like any old man Liddy had ever met. He was as tough as nails, and drove them relentlessly. At first Liddy had attempted to keep pace with him, but before very long he had collapsed down on to the sledge and allowed the dogs to carry him as well as their supplies.

Liddy had paid not just to kill the polar bear, but to enjoy the whole 'Eskimo' experience. He knew he wasn't supposed to call them Eskimos, but he could hardly help himself. Hadn't he grown up reading all about them? So far, however, he wasn't too impressed. The blubbery food Paul cooked was so revolting he'd given it to the dogs. In the dark of his tent, he'd chomped on a Power Bar and dreamed about McDonald's chicken nuggets. He was freezing, and hungry, and absolutely exhausted, and he missed having a television and a cell phone and doughnuts, but getting the bear would make it all worthwhile.

Sleep was impossible, with the wind howling and the yelping dogs. One of them had tried to bite a lump out of him when he'd gone for a pee. He had found Paul already standing outside, with his rifle raised to his shoulder.

'Something wrong?' Liddy had asked.

'Something spooked them,' said Paul.

Liddy just grunted and concentrated on trying to pee. It was so cold he was worried about *it* freezing up and dropping off. He washed his hands with snow and tramped back to the tent. He was paying far too much money to worry. The old man could stay on guard all night. Paul had the same rifle he had; there wasn't a creature on the planet could stand up to a Winchester Magnum. Besides, Paul was probably just playing it up, making like there was something out there. It was all part of the 'experience'.

But if those dogs don't quit hollering, I'll shoot one of them myself.

He wasn't an *entirely* unpleasant man, John Gordon Liddy III. He was just spoiled by civilization. If he had wanted to prove how brave he was to his friends, there were easier things he could have done, but no, here he was, on top of the world, a hundred miles from the nearest outpost and mere hours from death.

It was a little after noon when they saw the bear, about 1500 metres ahead, and facing away from them, halfway up a short incline. Paul raised his binoculars. Liddy preferred to study the beast through the telescopic sights of his rifle. His finger was already curling around the trigger. But he didn't shoot. The bear was still too far away, and he wanted the satisfaction of being close; he wanted to be able to look into the whites of his eyes as he killed him.

They left the dogs with the sledge, and moved cautiously forward. The bear was pawing at the snow, digging for something, its back to them, blissfully unaware that death was approaching – at least until the dogs behind them suddenly began to yelp again, probably having caught its scent. The bear turned slowly, its nose in the air. They were perhaps two hundred metres away. Liddy walked with his rifle to his shoulder and the creature in his sights, and now everything was perfect. He would have gone for a head shot, but he didn't want to spoil the look of the trophy he would soon have hanging on a wall at home. He was going to shoot it right in the heart.

Liddy began to squeeze the trigger, but just as he applied the final, killing pressure, Paul suddenly forced his barrel down. Liddy turned angrily to the Inuit. The old man was pointing to the left of the bear.

Liddy peered into the whiteness. At first he couldn't see anything. In truth he was finding it hard to take his eyes off the bear, which was now raised on its hindquarters, staring at them. Behind them the dogs continued to yelp and bark. But then he saw two disparate spots of movement. He raised his binoculars.

Cubs.

Two cute little balls of fur, frolicking in the snow, close to their den.

'We can't shoot her, Mr Liddy.'

'I got a licence, and I'm gonna shoot me a bear!'

'No, sir, terms of the licence forbids—'

'I don't care. I've come this far. I'm not going to walk away!'

Liddy snapped the rifle back to his shoulder and pulled the trigger. There was a loud crack. But he missed. Liddy had jerked at the trigger instead of gently squeezing, and the bullet had flown wide of its target.

'God damn it!'

Paul made another grab for the rifle, but Liddy threw him off. The old man tumbled away.

The bear had gathered the cubs to her now and was trying to shepherd them over the brow of the hill, but they thought it was just another game and tried to squeeze out of her grasp.

Liddy knew then that he would kill the cubs as well. He would have a whole family on his wall. He began to squeeze the trigger, but he hesitated at a noise from behind, some kind of snorting and growling.

One of the dogs must have gotten loose.

But then John Gordon Liddy III was hurled to the ground. He didn't even have time to scream as the huge creature pounced on him and sank its teeth into his throat and ripped the life from him.

Paul, thrown to one side by Liddy, had been separated from his rifle, and now it lay off to one side, on the far side of the creature. Its giant head turned towards him, it rose to its full height and it roared.

It was a polar bear, but fully twice the size of any he had ever seen.

Its jaw was a mass of sharp teeth, its muzzle soaked in blood.

All Paul's years of experience, and he hadn't realized that while they were hunting one creature, another was hunting them. A bear that had stepped out of the myths he had heard around the camp fire as a boy.

And now it was coming for him.

Chapter One

It was the worst weather England had experienced in twenty years. The snow descended overnight, surprising *everyone*, especially the weathermen. It lay twenty centimetres deep and more. The roads were impassable, the railways overwhelmed, aeroplanes grounded. Factories closed. Shops remained shuttered. Schools failed to open.

That is, except for St Mark's Retreat, a boarding school on the Pennines, that low and desolate mountain range which forms the backbone of the country. It was said that nothing would close St Mark's – it was a little world of its own, remote, self-sufficient, obstinate. St Mark's went defiantly about its business as if nothing was amiss. It was a school for boys whose parents thought they would benefit from a harsh regime and austere conditions. It was a school for boys who had nowhere else to go, for the unwanted, the abandoned and the lost. It was a school for boys whose parents were uninterested in their children, a school for boys whose parents were divorced but who couldn't agree on who should look after them. It was a school for orphans whose late parents had left behind money for their education or for boys who found themselves wards of the state. St Mark's was ancient and crumbling. St Mark's was tough. And on this day, freezing cold and assaulted by blizzards, St Mark's was on fire.

Really, *on fire*.

The West Wing was going up in flames. If it hadn't been for the blizzard, you could have seen the smoke and flames for miles.

The fire brigade, stranded in their stations, could do nothing to help.

Masters and boys formed human chains, passing buckets full of icy water along the lines in a desperate attempt to quell the inferno.

But still St Mark's burned.

And the reason it burned was because Michael Monroe was cold.

So he started a fire.

'What sort of a moron starts a fire in a school building?' Headmaster Nathaniel James bellowed when eventually the fire was put out, as much by the cascading snow as from the heroic efforts of teachers and pupils.

They were in the playground, the snow swirling around them.

Michael Monroe's response was, 'I was *really* cold.'

The Headmaster would probably have thumped him if there hadn't been so many witnesses. 'Get to my office, *boy*!' he yelled instead. He would probably thump him there.

But Michael Monroe didn't move.

'Are you deaf as well as stupid?!'

'Ahm, sir. Your office . . .'

Michael nodded towards the smouldering embers.

Headmaster James followed his gaze, and realization dawned.

'You . . . you . . . you . . . *ahghhh*!'

He threw his hands up in the air and stormed off. In a moment he was swallowed up by the snow.

Vincent Armoury, the head boy, stood at Michael's shoulder, shaking his head. 'You,' he said, 'are *so* dead.'

Twenty-four hours later the snow had stopped falling, but it lay defiantly on the ground, harder, frozen. In the towns and cities gritting machines had opened up the roads, but on the Pennines almost everything remained at a standstill. The fire brigade had just about made it out to inspect the ruined wing of the school, and then the police arrived, after hearing that the fire had been set deliberately. They were, thankfully, convinced that this was not a case of arson, but of stupidity. As they left, Michael, midway through a chemistry lesson, was summoned to the Head's makeshift office behind the kitchens. 'Take your books with you,' the teacher said, with a finality that suggested he wouldn't be back.

The Head had a file open on his desk. 'You've never really settled here, have you, Michael?'

Michael shrugged.

'In fact, you've never really settled anywhere. This is your sixth school in as many years. Now, I appreciate that you come from an, uhm, *unfortunate* background, but we have many pupils here who have had similar or indeed worse life experiences, and they haven't caused half the disruption that you have.'

Michael stared at the floor.

The Headmaster sighed. 'I have studied your reports, and I have spoken to your teachers. The general opinion is that you're a smart boy, but you don't apply yourself. You have an athletic build, but you don't participate in team sports. You are a teenager, and I accept that with that there comes a certain amount of what one might call *attitude*. But you have more attitude than any six teenage boys combined. You have been disruptive, you have been lazy, you have been disrespectful, you are clearly bereft of common sense. Have you anything to say for yourself?'

'My mother says if you've nothing nice to say, say nothing.'

The Head's eyes flared for a moment, but quickly softened. 'Your mother,' he said quietly, 'is no longer with us.'

'She said it before she left us.'

The Head took a deep breath. 'You've caused hundreds of thousands of pounds' worth of damage. Have you anything to say about *that*?'

Michael studied the Head. He was a thin man, with thinning hair, and thin lips.

'I was cold.'

'You were *cold*?'

'Yes. The heat in the radiators was *inadequate*.'

'*Inadequate?* Who are you to decide what is or isn't inad—'

'It was the coldest day of the year and there was barely any heat. It was definitely inadequate.'

'You—'

'I lit a fire in a fireplace. In a *hearth*. This stupid old school has dozens of them and we never use them. That's what they're *for*—'

'That's what—'

'Let me finish.' The Headmaster's mouth dropped open in astonishment. 'It was a perfectly in-control fire. It's not my fault that you're too cheap to have the chimneys cleaned properly. It's not my fault the chimney caught fire and the roof caught fire and half the school burned down. If you turned the heat up a bit I wouldn't have needed to—'

'It's not your fault?!' the Head finally cut in. '*It's not my fault* is always the last recourse of the scoundrel! Instead of standing up and admitting your guilt like a man, you blame somebody else! You just don't understand, do you, Michael? Because of your selfishness a fire broke out that could very easily have killed any number of your fellow pupils! It's a miracle nobody died!'

'Well, if it's a miracle, then God meant it to happen, so perhaps you should celebrate it rather than try to persecute anyone, particularly me.'

This was the final straw. The Head closed the file.

'I was prepared to give you a chance,' he said gravely,

'but frankly, I don't think there's any hope for you. I have a responsibility to the boys here to keep them safe, and quite honestly, with someone as reckless as you have shown yourself to be, I don't think they are. You leave me no option but to expel you from St Mark's and return you to the care of the education authority. This will take me a little while to organize, but if I were you I would pack up your things and expect to be leaving school first thing in the morning. The minibus will take you as far as Uppermill Station, but that's where my responsibility for you ends. You have brought nothing but shame to yourself and to this school. Now get out of my office.'

Michael stood. He shook his head. 'You only had to turn the radiators up,' he said, 'but I suppose that would have been another miracle.' He turned on his heel and left the office, leaving the Head's mouth moving up and down, like a fish gasping for air.

Chapter Two

The following morning Michael threw his meagre belongings into his bag, hoisted it up on to his shoulders, and wordlessly left the dormitory. He waited downstairs in the reception area, which was only slightly blackened by smoke from the fire, and within ten minutes the minibus arrived from its garage behind the school. When he climbed on board, however, he was dismayed to find that half of the seats were already taken by members of the debating team, on their way to a competition, already whispering about him and sniggering.

He was neither sad nor happy to be leaving St Mark's. He hadn't meant any harm by lighting the fire, and didn't see how he could possibly have foreseen what would happen when he did. The problem hadn't been setting the fire, it had been the school's own lack of maintenance. He'd probably even done them a favour. Maybe they'd get their act together in the future. Nobody had actually died, and they could undoubtedly build a new West Wing – and perhaps a warmer one.

Uppermill Station was two miles from the school. When he arrived there officials from the local education authority would meet him. Ordinarily they would have driven up, but with the roads so bad locally the train was the only option. They would accompany him to some temporary accommodation in some vaguely familiar city until they could place him in a different boarding school.

'What are you looking at?' Michael snapped.

A boy a couple of seats ahead of him had glanced at him, but now quickly looked away.

Armoury, the head boy, gave him a filthy look. Michael stared him out. Armoury might be a big muscular jock, but he had no power now – Michael was no longer a pupil of St Mark's. Armoury gave a slight, condescending shake of his head before looking away again.

Michael turned to the window and watched the pristine countryside race by. He thought about his parents. He had quoted what his mother had said to the Headmaster, but he'd just made that up. In reality he could hardly remember either of them at all. He had only been six years old when they had died in a car crash abroad. He had just a vague impression of them. His mother with dark hair. His father laughing. But the actual details of their faces were fuzzy. In the background there was fire. And people screaming. He dreamt about them often, and always woke up suddenly, in a sweat. But he never screamed himself.

The minibus skidded suddenly to one side, slipping on the frozen road. The driver shouted jovially back, 'Fasten your seat belts!'

Except the minibus was just like St Mark's itself – old and decrepit. There were no seat belts.

They were coming down off the Pennines and the incline was severe, though broken by numerous curves in the road. They jerked forward as the driver cautiously applied the brakes, but there were still moments when Michael could feel the bus literally gliding across ice.

And then, as they approached the final sharp drop down to the main road below, they skidded again. The driver turned the wheel sharply, pulled the hand brake and slammed on the brakes, but it just made matters worse. The bus actually picked up speed. Everyone could clearly see what was coming, but it was as if they were careering towards the stone wall in slow motion. Michael braced himself for the crash – but it didn't come. Somehow the out-of-control vehicle managed to find a gap in the wall and instead burst through a hedge, dropping over a metre into a snow-covered field.

But it was no miracle escape.

The incline was still just as sharp, and instead of burying itself in the deep snow the bus continued to hurtle forward, throwing its passengers around, until finally it ran out of solid ground, leapt into the air and splashed nose first into a River Ryburn running deep and hard with melting snow.

Those who hadn't already been hurled out of their seats by the drop into the field were catapulted forward. The windscreen buckled and icy water cascaded in. As the front of the bus dropped deeper into the swollen river the driver was sucked out and instantly disappeared into the current.

And it was all remarkably quiet.

The boys had been shocked into a mad kind of silence.

As the front of the bus sank further, the back end rose up out of the water. Michael climbed over the backs of the seats and clawed his way towards the emergency exit at the back. He yanked at the bar keeping it closed, but it was stiff with disuse. Armoury was suddenly beside him, and together they managed to shift it and push the door open.

'Come on!' Michael shouted down the bus, waving the other boys towards him.

As they began to clamber back, hauling themselves up by the seat safety rails, Armoury stared out at the dark water racing past them. The river bank was about ten metres away.

'It's too deep!' he shouted. 'It's too fast! We'll never make the bank!'

Michael reached back and lifted a schoolbag. He threw it out into the water, and it was instantly flushed away. Armoury was right. But what choice did they have? If the bus shifted again, they could all be sucked under and have no chance at all. At least if they tried to get to the bank some of them might make it. His eye was caught by the schoolbag again – it had been swept almost thirty metres down the river, but was now out of the raging current and nestling in among a small outcrop of rocks.

It was exactly the inspiration he needed. 'There!' he shouted, pointing excitedly. 'If I can make it to there, and you lower them in one by one, I can catch them as they go past!'

'No!' Armoury shouted. 'It's too dangerous!'

Michael couldn't help laughing. 'And *this* isn't?'

Armoury gave him a grim smile and nodded.

They were probably doomed whatever they did, but at least this meant they were doing something rather than just hanging around waiting to drown.

Michael stared at the outcrop, breathing deeply. It was a huge risk. He would have to depend on the current taking him there, but he was ten times heavier than a schoolbag. If he was swept past, he would surely drown. And so would everyone on the bus.

He had no alternative.

Michael plunged headfirst into the river. It was like getting stabbed with a thousand knives at once. It tried to suck him down, but he kicked and he kicked and he fought because his life depended on it. He forced his head up out of the water and saw the outcrop racing towards him, but knew he was still too far away. He kicked again. When he was almost level he gave one final surging thrust. He just managed to catch hold of the outermost rock. But it was slippy and his fingers had no feeling left in them. He lost his grip and was almost yanked away, but his feet cracked against a boulder below and it gave him just a moment to push backwards against it, enough to make a second attempt on the rock. This time he got a proper hold of it and dragged himself painfully out of the torrent.

Michael collapsed across the dank outcrop. The icy waters had taken such a vice-like grip on his lungs that he could hardly breathe. But he forced himself to turn at the sound of screeching metal as the bus plunged further down. The boys were shouting and yelling and waving at him. Michael pulled himself up. He gave the thumbs-up to Armoury, who immediately lowered the first boy into the water and let go of him. In moments he was flushed along.

Michael stretched out over the closest rock just in time and grabbed the boy as he passed. He pulled him out and levered him up and over his shoulders until he could roll with his own body weight on to the drier rocks behind. He had scarcely let go of him when Armoury released the next boy. Michael caught him again and dragged him out. His arms were already like dead weights. His whole body was shuddering with the cold. But he had no choice but to dip into the river again as another boy sped towards him. Again and again he plunged his arms into the water, flat on his stomach, steadying himself with his feet against the base of the outcrop behind, catching every boy as he sped towards him.

After what felt like an eternity, only Armoury himself remained. He was bigger than the other boys, and Michael was completely exhausted, but one more effort and they would all, unbelievably, be safe. Armoury gave him the thumbs-up. But just as he was setting himself to plunge into the water, the bus shifted again, this time so violently that the exit door, which had been open at an angle, shuddered once and slammed closed, cracking off Armoury's head in the process and knocking him both unconscious and into the water. Without the forward thrust he'd been giving to the other boys, Armoury was too far out for Michael to grab and he could only watch, horrified, as the head boy was swept past.

Chapter Three

Michael was confused. He knew he was dead. *Obviously* he was dead. He had to be. He had thrown himself into the Ryburn to try and save Armoury, and that had been foolhardy in the extreme. He hadn't even properly thrown himself in – that suggested he'd had some kind of residual strength left in his frozen body. He had really just fallen in and almost immediately been sucked under. He remembered nothing after that. So he was definitely dead. Except that didn't explain why he was lying in a bed that looked suspiciously like the nurse's room at St Mark's, and certainly smelled like it. He scratched at his head, but in raising his arm realized that there was an IV drip attached to it. In the distance a bell sounded. He heard the thump-thump of hundreds of pairs of feet on old wooden steps and the frantic buzz of a swarm of boys talking at once.

'I'm not dead,' he said.

'No, you're not.'

Surprised, he twisted to his left. Vincent Armoury sat in a chair by his bed. He had a bandage around his head, but for another dead man, he was looking pretty healthy. Michael pushed himself up into a sitting position.

'You—'

'You saved my life.'

'I don't remember.'

'You pulled me out of the river, unconscious. You gave me the kiss of life. You saved twelve other boys. You even dived back into the bus to look for the driver. He washed up further down the river, absolutely fine. But you did it. You were running around like a man possessed. You kept everyone moving so they wouldn't freeze to death. You kept everyone's spirits up until help arrived. Then you collapsed. They brought you back here because the road to the hospital is still impassable. Michael Monroe, you're a bloody hero.'

Michael blinked at him. He made a face. 'I kissed you?'

Armoury smiled. 'I won't tell anyone. But I should go and tell the Head you're awake.' He stood up. 'I think he's reconsidering expelling you. There are a couple of photographers and a camera crew hanging around wanting to get pictures of you as well. You'll be in all the news . . .' He paused then, his attention drawn to the window. Michael had been aware of a clattering sound gradually becoming louder. Armoury crossed the room, pulled open an ancient pair of lace curtains, and opened the window. The noise became *really* loud, and, unmistakably, that of a helicopter.

Michael peered beyond Armoury. It wasn't just a little bee-like chopper for a couple of people coming in to land in the school grounds, but a huge machine like the army might use to transport troops or equipment. Except this one wasn't camouflaged, it was white with red lettering down the side.

'SOS,' said Armoury. 'What on earth are they doing here?'

'SOS?'

'SOS. You know. They save people.'

'They're a bit late,' said Michael.

He had heard of SOS, the distress signal, but not *this* SOS. And he didn't much care who they were. He didn't think 'they' were here to save anyone anyway. More likely some anxious parent who worked for SOS, having heard either about the accident or the fire that had destroyed half the school, was coming to check on their precious offspring.

As Armoury left the room Michael fell back on his pillow. The Head was reconsidering his expulsion? He was a hero? He had kissed a boy? He didn't believe the first two, and he was doing his best to forget the third. He didn't care one way or the other about being expelled. St Mark's wasn't any worse or any better than any of the other schools he'd been expelled from over the years. And he certainly wasn't a hero. If he had gone out of his way to save Armoury, and then returned to the water to look for the missing driver, then it was because his brain was half frozen and he was temporarily deranged. Who, in their right mind, would attempt any of that?

He closed his eyes, and was just slipping into a pleasant dream when the door was suddenly flung open and the nurse marched in, followed by the Head, accompanied by another man he didn't recognize.

The Head stood at the foot of the bed and beamed proudly. 'This is the boy – this is our young hero!'

The other man studied Michael. 'I heard he was being expelled.'

'No! Not a bit of it! Purely a misunderstanding!'

Michael guessed the man to be about fifty. He had a

thin face, a goatee beard and grey-flecked short hair. He was wearing black jeans and a zip-up jacket with lots of pockets.

'I'd think I'd prefer to speak to Michael alone.'

The Head looked surprised. 'I'm not sure if that would be appropriate. These days—'

'Mr James, may I remind you that I am considering paying for the replacement of your West Wing? The wing you neglected to take out insurance for?'

The Head cleared his throat. 'Of course. I'll, uhm, just be outside.'

'Go further,' said the man.

The Head, not looking happy at all, swept out of the room, taking the nurse with him. The man waited until their footsteps receded before dropping into the chair Armoury had recently vacated. He propped his legs up on the bed and breezily asked how Michael was doing.

'Fine.' The man nodded. And sat there. Looking at him. Michael just wanted to roll over and go back to sleep. 'I'm sorry, but is there something I can help you with?'

'Aren't you curious? I've just arrived in a big helicopter and come straight to see you.'

'No,' said Michael. 'I'm tired.'

'I understand that, of course. Obviously you know who I am, I just thought I'd—'

'No, I don't.'

'You don't recognize my face?'

'No. Now if you don't mind I—'

'Do you not watch television?'

'Not much, no.'

'Read papers, surf the internet? You really don't recognize me?'

'Are you wanted for murder, or something?'

'The Head said you had a smart mouth. He thought it was a bad thing. But I happen to think it's a sign of intelligence. God knows mine has gotten me into enough trouble.' He tapped himself on the chest. 'Jimmy Kincaid. *Doctor* Jimmy Kincaid. Dr Jimmy, saving the planet one campaign at a time? SOS? You must know all about SOS?' But he could tell that Michael didn't have a clue. 'Well, we can soon rectify that. As for why I'm here, well, I heard about you saving those boys. It was certainly very heroic, but also . . . surprising. Out of character.'

'What do you mean *out of character*? How on earth would you know?'

'Well, because, I keep track of you.'

'*Me?*'

'Yes, of course. I keep tabs on all my children.'

Michael just stared at him.

'Relax, kiddo, I don't mean *literally*. I mean . . . what do I mean? Well, I should really tell you from the start. Have you heard about the dolphins? No, of course you haven't. Let me tell you about the dolphins, and then we can get on to, you know . . . being one of my children.'

Michael nodded. Then he said, 'If you could just excuse me for one moment?' He lifted the phone sitting on the bedside locker. He calmly pressed the zero to put him through to the school secretary's office. When it was picked up he suddenly bellowed, 'HELP! There's a nutter on the loose up here!'

Chapter Four

Dr Jimmy Kincaid calmly reached across and took the phone out of Michael's hand. There was an authority to him as he spoke quietly into the mouthpiece. 'This is Dr Kincaid. Everything up here is absolutely fine. No, you have a good day as well.'

He replaced the phone and sat back in his chair, clasped his hands and said, 'I just want you to listen to me. Then you can make your own mind up.'

'About *what*?'

'Well, I'll get to that.'

'Right. *OK*. If you insist.'

He was, *of course*, curious. He just didn't like to admit it.

'*OK*. Michael. Back in the 1980s, I used to be a pop star. Jimmy Kincaid. Or my fans knew me as Jimmy K. I've had many hits.'

'Uhuh.'

This man was clearly *bonkers*.

'I toured the world, I played in huge arenas, I took every drug known to man, I had ten thousand girlfriends, thirteen houses, thirty cars, I spent many many millions of pounds. But was I happy?'

'No . . . ?'

'Of course I was happy! I had everything I'd ever dreamt of. It was fantastic!'

'But . . . ?'

'Why does there have to be a but? I had the time of my life! But, OK, there *is* a *but*. I got tired of it all. I had fifty million dollars in the bank, and I'd run out of things to spend it on. Because I was addicted to drugs, my concert tours were cancelled, and the music I made was awful. It no longer sold. I was washed up. *Rich*, but washed up. I decided to end it all. Kill myself.'

'Have you come here to cheer me up?' Michael asked. 'Because you're not doing a very good job.'

'Just . . . *listen*.' Michael sighed. 'OK, I was going to kill myself. I was at my place in Florida. I decided I'd swim out into the Atlantic, keep swimming until I couldn't swim any further, just drift away. I swam for about ten minutes – I wasn't that far out – but I wasn't fit, I was getting tired. I knew it wouldn't be too long before I was exhausted. Then a dolphin started swimming beside me. I shouted at him to go away. I wanted to die alone.'

'Did he shout anything back?'

Dr Kincaid ignored him. 'But then a second dolphin appeared, then a third and a fourth, and pretty soon there was a whole school of them around me. I screamed at them to leave me alone, but instead they just got closer and closer until I could hardly swim at all. They began to circle me, going faster and faster, and they started to beat their tails furiously into the water, churning it all up. I just thought, dolphins are supposed to be these lovely, friendly, intelligent creatures, and here they are trying to kill me!'

'So why didn't you let them?'

'Because I didn't want to be murdered by dolphins! I wanted it to be my choice! They just wouldn't leave me alone. I was absolutely exhausted, could hardly kick my legs to tread water, but now I'd gone the opposite way – I was suddenly determined to survive. I tried to break out of the circle, threw myself at them, but they wouldn't let me through, kept beating those tails, forcing me back. They kept me prisoner out there for nearly twenty minutes. They were so organized. When one swam off because he was tired, another was ready to take his place. Then, just at the point where I really was about to drown, they just suddenly swam away. Every single one of them just left me there. All I wanted to do then was to get back on dry land. I wanted to live.

'The thing is, Michael, I made it back, I dragged myself up on to that beach, and I flopped down barely able to breathe. And then a helicopter landed beside me. And I thought great, it's the paparazzi, going to take photos of this poor, bloated rock star exhausted by his little swim – but it wasn't, it was the police. They patrol up and down the coast looking for drug runners. They ran up to me and said they'd been flying over and saw what happened and they'd never seen anything like it in their lives – and I said, I know, those dolphins tried to kill me! And they looked at me and shook their heads and said, no, the dolphins saved my life. They realized then that I couldn't have seen what they'd seen from above. They saw the dolphins swimming around me – and also a Great White Shark. The dolphins had formed a protective circle around me, beating their tails to try and frighten the shark away. When it wouldn't go, they took turns to attack it. The dolphins weren't swimming away exhausted, they were going into battle with a Great White. To save me! The police reckoned the shark killed two of them before it eventually gave up and swam away, and only then did the dolphins let me go. Do you understand what I'm saying, Michael? Those dolphins saved my life. They sacrificed themselves to save *me*.'

'Really? Seriously?'

'Hand on heart. And I sat there on the sand, absolutely stunned. The dolphins didn't know me, they didn't know my music or how wealthy or famous I was or what type of a man I was, they just protected me. And do you know something, Michael? It changed me. It made me realize how stupid I'd been. How precious life actually is. There on that beach I got to thinking about all the people in the world who struggle every day to hang on to their lives, and I'd almost thrown mine away. All those people who survive tidal waves and earthquakes and civil wars. It made me think about all the creatures in the world and how fantastic they are, not just the dolphins, but all of them: gorillas, lions, tigers, eagles . . .'

'Sharks?'

'Yes, even sharks. All the creatures we seem intent on wiping out, whether through hunting or destroying their natural habitat or pollution or global warming . . . I just knew suddenly what I had to do. I had millions and millions in the bank, but I was just frittering it away on nothing. What if I could do something that made a real difference? Michael, there are hundreds of charities out there, thousands, but I didn't just want to hand over a pile of money and walk away, I wanted to actually do something myself, something I could be sure would make a real difference. The charities all do fantastic jobs. But many of them are slow, they take weeks or months to take action, they rely on the public sending them money, they rely on governments allowing them into their countries, the right paperwork coming through, when every second they waste, through no fault of their own, is costing lives. What I wanted to do was to help in the way that the dolphins had helped me – an instantaneous reaction. I mean, what if the dolphins had spotted the shark about to attack me – then held a committee meeting to decide what they should do?'

'You'd be dead.'

'Exactly. And *that's* why I founded SOS. I bought helicopters, I recruited a crack team of experts, and now that's what we do. We fly where we're needed exactly when we're needed and don't stop to ask for permission.'

'Look, I'm sure this is all fascinating. But what on

earth has it got to do with *me*?'

'Forgive me. I do ramble. OK. We've had successes, we've had failures. Twelve years ago there was a civil war in the Balkans, a particularly bloody one. Both sides told us they would shoot down our helicopters if we entered their airspace. There were civilians trapped in no-man's land. Nobody was willing to help them. So we went in. We were only on the ground for a few minutes. We flew as many out as we could. There were many orphans, and you were one of them.'

'*Me?*'

'Yes, son. Nobody ever knew what happened to your parents. I'm sorry. We put you into our adoption programme here in England, but it seems that from an early age you've been quite . . . difficult, so when that proved impossible, and fostering didn't work out either . . . well, we've been paying for your various boarding schools for the past eight or nine years.'

'*You've* been paying?'

'You'll forgive me if I haven't been in touch before, but I have been busy saving the world. However, it is part of the SOS ethos not to just abandon the people we rescue, but to look after them and support them. The Headmaster here is obliged to send us reports on you every month, or when there's something urgent he feels we should know. So your heroism was very quickly brought to our attention, as was your ability to burn things down. So I decided it was time to take a proper look at you.'

'*Why?*'

'Well, it seems to me that any boy who can dive repeatedly into dangerous, frozen waters to save helpless children doesn't need to be wasting his time at some second-rate boarding school – he needs to be doing something that better suits his abilities. He needs to join SOS.'

Chapter Five

Dr Kincaid looked crestfallen when Michael told him that he had absolutely no intention of joining SOS. He had dived into the river because his brain was frozen and he'd no idea what he was doing. If he'd been in his right mind, and been able to weigh up the dangers, there was *no way* he would have gone in. He just wanted a quiet life. Why on earth would he want to put himself into further danger, which was what SOS seemed to be all about?

Dr Kincaid made several attempts to convince him, emphasizing not only the importance of what his organization did, but the excitement that came with it.

'You're a teenager! Wouldn't you rather be saving the planet than be a prisoner in some dreary boarding school?'

'No,' said Michael.

Eventually Dr Kincaid gave up. He stood up and extended his hand. 'Well, it's your decision.'

Michael shook it. 'Sorry,' he said.

'Don't worry about it.' Kincaid gave him a long, steady look before he said, 'What you did out on the river was fantastic. You may not realize it yet, but you have something in you, something special. Don't forget that. And maybe one day you'll put it to good use.'

Dr Kincaid nodded once, then spun on his heel and left the room, leaving the door ajar.

Michael slumped back on his pillows, but before he could gather his thoughts, the Head stepped silently back into the room.

'I thought he told you to—'

'Ah, Monroe, he fell for the oldest trick in the book.' The Head cracked a foot down hard on the wooden floor, then rapidly repeated the action half a dozen times, but making each step just slightly lighter, so that it sounded as if he was walking away. 'I was next door the whole time!'

The Head turned to the window, placed two hands on the sill, and looked down at the SOS helicopter parked in the middle of one of the school's snow-covered rugby pitches. He shook his head.

'Joining SOS? I don't think so. They're glory hunters, that's all they are, interfering where they're not wanted, and he's the worst of them. Nothing more than a jumped-up little singer. Just because he's sold a few records he thinks whatever he says and does is somehow important. I'll tell you what he has, Monroe, he has money, but you will learn that money doesn't buy you class. That only comes with a good education and by mixing with the right calibre of people.'

The Head finally turned from the window and clasped his hands behind his back.

'Right now that fool is downstairs with my secretary writing a cheque to rebuild the West Wing you burned down. What I say is that a fool and his money are soon parted. Now, you seem to have recovered rather well from your ordeal. I think it's time you returned to class. Yes, my boy, I have decided to give you a second chance – so please don't let me down. I'll send the nurse in to remove your drip. Your uniform is all freshly cleaned, so get yourself dressed and let's forget all this nonsense about SOS! Now I've an assembly to take – outside, thanks to you!'

As soon as the Head swept out of the room, Michael threw back the bed covers and sat up. He felt a little bit dizzy. He cautiously got to his feet, then shuffled across to the window, pulling the drip, which was attached to a wheeled tripod, with him. The glass had partially steamed up with the Head's breath. Michael rubbed at it with his pyjama sleeve. Now he could see properly out over the school grounds – the SOS helicopter to the left on the rugby field, on the right the boys gathered in military fashion in the snow before a makeshift stage, with a small keyboard and amplifier off to one side in front of Mr Christie, the music teacher. Dr Kincaid stood between the assembled boys and the helicopter, waiting to greet the Head as he moved down the steps and then ponderously across the snow. They shook hands. Something was said and they both laughed, though neither of them looked like they meant it. Dr Kincaid turned to his helicopter, the Head to his assembled boys.

Michael stared left, and stared right.

He watched as Dr Kincaid boarded the helicopter and the blades slowly began to rotate.

He watched as the Head took to his stage and nodded at Mr Christie to begin playing, and also made a little turning motion with his hand to get him to turn up the volume.

Michael had a sudden churning sensation in his stomach.

His heart began to race.

He wasn't ill: it was adrenaline, coursing through him like electricity. Standing there in the window, it was as if he was looking at a map of his future life. He had come to a crossroads and had to decide which direction to go in.

Rejoin the school, get a traditional education, perhaps acquire some 'class' along the way.

Or join SOS, and fly off to dangerous foreign countries, into war zones and earthquakes, and battle to save endangered species.

The clatter of the rotor blades was getting louder. So was the sound of Mr Christie's keyboard, almost as if a challenge had been issued. It was also joined by the Head's booming voice as he enthusiastically led the boys into the school song.

What had the Head said?

You have brought nothing but shame to yourself and to this school.

And what had Dr Kincaid said?

You may not realize it yet, but you have something in you, something special.

Nobody had ever told him he had something special.

What if he really did? How would he ever really find

out what he was capable of, stuck here with a ridiculous snob like the Headmaster?

Suddenly Michael *knew*.

He would never know who his real parents were, and now, suddenly, after dreaming about them for as long as he could remember, it didn't seem to matter. SOS had adopted him, educated him, kept a distant eye on him, and now it was . . . it was his *destiny* to join them. He had never felt part of anything, never known a family, but now Dr Kincaid was offering him one, with added thrills, adventure and danger.

And he absolutely wanted it.

But Dr Kincaid and SOS were about to fly out of his life.

Michael looked down at the IV needles taped to the inside of his wrist. In an instant he tore the strip holding them in place off his skin and then gently eased them out of his vein. A little blood spurted out.

He looked at his shoes and uniform at the bottom of the bed, then back to the helicopter, the blades getting faster and faster.

There wasn't time!

Michael turned and charged barefoot from the room.

The nurse was just coming down the hall towards

him. She shouted something and tried to stop him, but he bolted past. He got to the top of the creaking wooden staircase and bounded down it with one hand on the rail, taking the steps six at a time. He tore across the floor of the entrance hall, slipping and sliding on sludgy footprints. He bounded out of the front doors and down the steps and across the car park, not even noticing the snow on his bare feet as the icy wind ripped his flimsy pyjama top open.

The helicopter was finally lifting off.

'No!' Michael screamed. 'Wait!'

But his words were blown away.

If had looked to his right he would also have seen the Head angrily waving, his mouth working in anger, and the boys turning from their hymn to watch.

The helicopter doors were still half open.

He ran almost bent double against the downdraught.

He could hear nothing beyond the blades.

Not the Headmaster screaming.

Not the boys breaking ranks and cheering him on. Boys who didn't even know why he was running, who only knew that he was escaping from St Mark's.

Michael launched himself at the opening. His hands struggled for an endless second to hold on to something, but there was nothing and he began to fall back – until one hand was grabbed, then the other and he was hauled up and into the helicopter. He tumbled forward, rolled over and lay on his back, breathing hard as the helicopter rose into the sky.

He opened his eyes, scarcely able to believe what he had done, that he had made it.

Dr Kincaid was smiling down at him. 'I knew you would come,' he said, 'and we wouldn't have gone without you.'

He pulled Michael to his feet. He guided him across the floor of the helicopter and lowered him into a seat.

'Buckle up. This could get rocky!'

Michael grinned at him as he scrambled to secure his belt, still trying to catch his breath. As the helicopter banked his gaze fell on the school grounds below. Some of the boys were now running across the rugby field, gazing up after him, and even as they began to recede he realized that they were the same boys he had pulled from the icy river, and most noticeable among them all was Armoury, waving up.

Chapter Six

The helicopter was in the air for less than thirty minutes before it swept down out of the clouds on to an airfield. Michael had barely put his feet on the ground before he was whisked off in a Land Cruiser with blacked-out windows towards a drab-looking combination of hangar, warehouse and office block.

This was SOS HQ. The hub of all of its activities.

There were huge television screens showing maps of the world and locations where the organization was currently working. Video clips of disasters or dictators were playing above and around him. There were vast banks of computers and what seemed like hundreds of operators working feverishly at them. People were rushing about, talking into headsets or shouting at colleagues.

Michael felt excited by the size and scope of it all,

but also a little lost. When he finally thought to turn and ask Dr Kincaid what he was supposed to be doing he had disappeared. He didn't know if they'd simply forgotten him or deliberately left him behind. He didn't know where to turn or who to ask, and he was just contemplating quietly making his way back out into the fresh air when a girl suddenly appeared before him and snapped:

'Monroe?'

Michael nodded. She looked him up and down, and appeared distinctly unimpressed. He guessed she was roughly his age; she had black shoulder-length hair and blue eyes. She was wearing black jeans and a white T-shirt.

'Walk this way.'

She led him along a narrow corridor between the computer terminals and then up a set of stairs into a suite full of medical equipment. She pointed at a bed and said, 'Lie there, face down, and drop your trousers.'

'Excuse me?'

She was opening a cabinet on the wall. When she turned she had a very large hypodermic needle in her hand. She raised an eyebrow.

'Just get on the bed!' she barked.

Michael moved reluctantly to the bed. He put his

hands on the white sheet covering a slim mattress and pushed. He wasn't the slightest bit interested in how soft or springy it was. He was just desperately stalling. She was *his age*. She *couldn't* be a doctor, not unless she was some kind of genius. But she had a definite air of authority about her.

'I haven't got all day!'

Michael swallowed. He straightened, took a deep breath, then very quickly unbuttoned his trousers, pulled them down to just beneath his bum and lay down on the bed.

'Pants as well!'

Michael closed his eyes, and lowered them.

'This is going to hurt,' said the girl. 'Try not to cry.'

'What . . . what's this in aid of?'

'Diphtheria, tetanus, hepatitis, typhoid, tuberculosis, rabies . . . that's the first one, at least. Now brace yourself.'

Michael squeezed his eyes shut even harder and tensed himself for the pain.

A cough from the door stopped her in her tracks. Michael opened his eyes and turned his head to see a man with close-cropped grey hair in a white coat and with a stethoscope around his neck. He was also wearing a rather puzzled expression.

'Katya,' he said, 'what do you think you're doing?'

Michael's head screwed around further. Instead of finding her poised over him with the hypodermic, she had a mobile phone in her hand, and positioned in such a way that there was absolutely no doubt about what she was doing.

She was taking a video of his bum.

Michael scrambled on to his back and pulled up his trousers as fast as he possibly could.

Katya let out a sadistic laugh and skipped merrily towards the door.

'Aw, Dr Faustus, just making the new boy welcome!'

She squeezed past him and disappeared.

Mortified, and angry with it, Michael jumped off the bed, determined to give chase, but Dr Faustus held up his hand. 'Not so fast!'

Michael hesitated.

He wasn't used to letting anyone get away with anything, and it had got him into trouble a hundred times. But this was his first day with SOS; he was starting a new life. He had to control his temper. *Had to.* Michael glared after Katya, but stayed where he was. He wouldn't forget what she'd done, and one day, when she was least expecting it, he would get his own back on her.

Dr Faustus now had the hypo Katya had set down in his hand, but was changing the needle. He turned to Michael and raised an eyebrow.

Michael sighed heavily, dropped his trousers again, and lay back down on the bed.

Dr Faustus nodded for a moment and then said, 'This is for your arm.'

Chapter Seven

For several long moments Michael didn't know where he was. There was an alarm sounding, but everything was black. He was in bed. He sat up and winced. His arms and legs ached. He must have had a dozen injections and a whole battery of blood tests. He rubbed his knuckles into his brow and tried to remember. Yes – late last night he had been shown to this tiny room on the top floor of the warehouse complex, bare but for a bed and side locker, and told to get some sleep. He had said there was no way he was going to sleep, there was so much he still needed to find out about SOS and its headquarters and its people . . . but he must have gone out like a light as soon as his head touched the pillow.

Now there were charging footsteps up and down the corridor outside his room. It sounded like a fire alarm, but he could smell nothing burning. He dragged himself up and felt along the wall until he found the switch for the bare bulb hanging down from the ceiling. He opened the door and peered out. One of the computer guys was just hurrying past.

'Hey – what's going on?'

'The Artists are being scrambled!'

'The what . . . ?'

'No time!' the programmer yelled before breaking into a sprint.

Michael closed the door, confused. But there was no question of lying down again. Something was happening, and he was determined to be part of it. He pulled on his T-shirt and trousers and laced up his boots as quickly as he could with all his aches and pains, then exited the room and made his way down to the ground floor – directly into a cacophony of sound and a kaleidoscope of colour.

The massive screens were showing satellite maps, thermal images, reports from dozens of different news and weather channels, all in a bewildering array of languages. Several video conferences were taking place at once and most of the computer operators seemed to be jumping up and down shouting out random sequences of numbers. There was just too much information coming at Michael at once for him to get a firm grip on what was happening. He spotted Dr Kincaid walking back and forth, urgently talking into a mobile phone. Behind him two men identically dressed in black were staring up at a map and pointing. One of them huge and powerful-looking, the other small and shaven-headed. Bailey, the helicopter pilot who'd brought him to the SOS headquarters the previous day, winked at him as he crossed in front of him. Then Dr Faustus came rushing past, no longer wearing his white doctor's coat but zipping himself into an identical black uniform.

'Dr Faustus! What's going on?'

The doctor held up his hands, indicating that he didn't have time to explain. But then he stopped, looked around him and barked out, 'Katya!'

The girl, still wearing a white T-shirt and with her black hair caught up in a ponytail, was a little to Michael's left, leaning over a computer operator's shoulder and intently watching his monitor.

She didn't even look round. 'Yes?'

'Brief Michael on what's happening.'

Now she did. 'What? *Why?*'

'Just do it!'

Dr Faustus hurried on. Katya glared across at Michael

before returning her gaze to the monitor. After a few seconds she looked up again and growled, '*Well?*'

Michael didn't want to even be in the same building with her, but he was desperate to know what was going on. He moved across and stood on the other side of the computer operator. Katya jabbed a finger at the image on screen: a satellite image of what appeared to be a snow-covered island.

'Recognize it?' Katya asked.

How on earth could he recognize it? It could be *anywhere*. Rather than snap something at her, he just stared intensely at the screen.

'It's Baring Island, in the Northwest Territories,' said Katya.

'I was just thinking that.'

'So you know where the Northwest Territories are?'

His mind raced: had he *ever* heard of the Northwest Territories?

Probably not.

'Of *course*.'

'Where?'

At any other time of year he might have been able to guess, but with the British Isles and probably most of Europe under snow, it could be *anywhere*. Was the clue in the name? Northwest? Northwest of what? His eyes flitted up: he saw snow on one screen, a snowmobile on another, then there was the briefest glimpse of a red and white flag fluttering behind a reporter as he delivered a piece to camera. A leaf in the centre. That was . . . that was . . . that was . . .

'Canada, *obviously*,' he guessed.

'Just over two hours ago a rocket launched out of Cape Canaveral in Florida carrying the Eden satellite. You've heard of the Eden satellite?'

'Remind me.'

'It was to collect precise measurements of greenhouse gases and pinpoint global warming in the Earth's atmosphere. It's the first of its type, designed to gather evidence that nobody can argue with.'

'That's it. What about it?'

'Three minutes after launch, just as the satellite was about to separate from the rocket, it suddenly went off radar.'

'Off . . . ?'

'NASA says it exploded on the edge of space and small pieces of harmless debris have been coming down over Canada. But we were monitoring the launch and we don't think it even got that far. We believe it could still be in one piece, and our best estimate is that it has crash-landed somewhere in the

Northwest Territories, probably on Baring Island.'

'OK. And why is that any of our business?'

Katya rolled her eyes. 'What?'

'You know, why are we interested?'

'*We?*'

'SOS.'

'Oh yeah. I forgot. You think you're one of us now, don't you?'

Their eyes locked – and stayed that way until the computer operator, looking from one to the other, decided to intervene. He tapped on his monitor and said, 'Because Baring Island is the biggest national park on the planet. If a rocket containing thousands of litres of highly toxic hydrazine propellant crash-lands there it could devastate the environment.'

Michael broke eye contact with Katya and looked at the screen. 'I don't understand – why would NASA say it had broken up if it hasn't? Surely they know more than—'

'Because it was shot down, you idiot!'

Katya grabbed her jacket off the desk and stormed away.

Michael looked at the programmer. 'Is she kidding?'

'Does she look like she's kidding?'

'But why would anyone shoot—?'

The programmer held up his hands. 'Don't ask me, I only push buttons.'

Michael took a deep breath and went after her. As he did he saw other figures were moving ahead of her, all in the same direction: Dr Faustus, Dr Kincaid, the helicopter pilot Bailey, and two others he didn't recognize. Dr Kincaid led them through a set of doors. Michael only hesitated for a moment after they swung shut behind Katya. He pushed through and caught up with her just as she approached the end of a narrow corridor.

'Katya?'

She glanced behind her. 'What do you want?' she snapped impatiently. 'You're not supposed to be—'

'You were told to brief me.'

'I did!'

'Where are you going? What are they doing?'

'It's none of your business!'

She spun away. Michael followed her through another door which opened on a different part of the hangar. At one end he could see the Hercules. But here, right in front of him, there was an entirely different kind of aircraft. A sleek and very modern-looking private jet with a very small SOS painted on its side. The steps were down, and Dr Kincaid was just boarding.

Having had no success with Katya, Michael found himself blurting out:

'Dr Kincaid?'

Dr Kincaid stopped in the doorway. The others, taken by surprise, bunched up behind him on or around the steps. They all looked at Michael.

Katya said, 'I'm sorry, I told him to—'

But the SOS founder cut in. 'Yes, Michael?'

'What . . . where . . . are you going to Baring Island?'

'That's the plan.'

'Can I . . . would it be poss . . . is there any way . . .'

Dr Kincaid smiled. 'He wants to come too.'

They *all* smiled. Michael felt about eight years old and eight centimetres high.

'Yes.'

'And what exactly do you think you could contribute to the Action Response Team?'

Action Response Team – that's what the programmer had meant by 'the Artists'.

'I . . . don't know . . .'

Dr Kincaid stepped slightly to one side to allow 'the Artists' to enter the jet. As he did he nodded at each one, before looking back to Michael.

'Could you, for example, fly a jet with the skill of a fighter pilot, or land a helicopter on the eye of a needle in the middle of a hurricane, like Bailey?'

Michael shook his head.

Dr Faustus stepped up to the doorway.

'Could you, for example, carry out a kidney transplant in the middle of a jungle while under constant gunfire, and with a bullet in your own leg?'

Michael shook his head.

As Dr Faustus ducked into the body of the jet, the huge man Michael had spotted earlier mounted the steps. He had muscles that were bigger than Michael's head. He had action and power and courage written all over him.

'Could you face down a rampaging mob with nothing more than your fists, and defuse a land mine at the same time? Mr Crown can.'

Michael didn't even bother shaking his head.

'Or perhaps you have mastered twenty-six languages like Monsieur Bonsoir, here?' The small, shaven-headed man Michael had seen studying a map with Mr Crown was next on board. 'Or can plan something as complicated as the invasion of Normandy on the back of a napkin in sixteen minutes while being assaulted by a plague of locusts?'

Finally Katya stepped up into the doorway. She was just pulling on her black jacket and zipping it up. Her uniform was now exactly the same as every other member of the SOS Action Response Team.

'Or you might even have the skills of young Katya here, our trainee. She flies as well as Bailey, she has nearly as many languages as Bonsoir, and in a tight corner she could probably knock the blocks off as many ninjas as you care to throw at her.'

Katya disappeared through the door.

'Or maybe even you could do as little as I do – which is talk up a storm to popes and presidents, and pay for it all?'

Michael just stood there. Dr Kincaid raised his hands helplessly before turning to enter the body of the aircraft. But then he stopped and looked back. There was a puzzled expression on his face. He clicked his fingers.

'There's something I've forgotten. What was it? Oh – it'll come to me.' He clicked again, then opened his hand and began to count off his fingers one by one. 'I have the pilot, I have the doctor, I have the bomb disposal expert, I have the languages and logistics guy and the trainee, and I have myself – I can hardly forget myself, can I? But what have I forgotten?' He clicked once more. 'It's coming to me . . . it's coming . . . oh yes, I have it! I haven't got a fella who's expert at nothing but could probably make himself useful making coffee. Do you know anyone like that?'

Michael was on board in three seconds flat.

Chapter Eight

Michael was making himself coffee when Bailey joined him in the galley at the back of the jet. 'Not sleeping?' the pilot asked.

Michael shook his head. Everyone else had been zonked out for hours, but he felt like his brain was going to explode, there were so many thoughts running through it. Had someone really shot down the Eden satellite? Who? Why? Was NASA really covering it up? How was SOS going to find it before NASA? Was anyone else looking for it? Did it have a tracking device? Just how good were the Artists? How could he ever be expert enough in anything to become one of them? How come Katya was so good at everything? Why did she hate him? Did she have a sad story like his, or was she just a horrible human being? How come Faustus and Bonsoir had such unusual names? Were they nicknames? Or did they also have a mysterious past that led them to adopt unlikely monikers? And why was he here at all? All he had done was save some stupid kids from a river – how did that justify bringing him across the Atlantic slap bang into the middle of a hunt for a missing satellite? What could he contribute, beyond coffee? He had tasted his own coffee and it really wasn't *that* good.

Bailey was looking a little surprised.

Michael swallowed. 'Did I say any of that out loud?'

Bailey laughed. 'Hey, don't worry, kid,' he said, 'I was like this, first time, couldn't sit still. It *is* exciting. It's just that these guys . . .' and he nodded at the Artists sleeping in their luxurious leather chairs, '. . . have done it so many times before. In this line, you take your rest where you can get it. I'm sure all your questions will be answered as we go along. But one thing, Dr Kincaid brought you along for a reason, and even if he isn't quite sure of it himself, I'm sure it'll reveal itself at the right time.'

Bailey continued to stand there looking at him. He had an expectant look on his face. After a few moments Michael said, 'What?'

Bailey nodded down at the coffee pot.

'Oh! Right. My primary responsibility.'

He quickly began to pour Bailey a cup – but then stopped, as a thought suddenly struck him. He glanced up. 'Yours is a nickname as well, isn't it? I thought Bailey was just an ordinary surname, but it's not, it means . . . you bail out of aircraft.'

'You've got it. I've bailed out of six jets and nine helicopters over the years, yet here I am, good as new.'

'And the jets and helicopters?'

'Exploded in balls of fire, mostly. Although there was one that just had a flat tyre and I overreacted a bit.' He gave a little shrug. 'This is a dangerous business. If you fly by the seat of your pants, sometimes you land on your arse. You try flying into a volcano or a hurricane, sooner or later you're gonna run into problems. Good news is I haven't killed anyone. Yet.'

Michael had an even more worrying thought. 'Ahm . . . who exactly is flying us at the moment?'

Bailey looked puzzled. 'Us? Isn't . . . ? Sometimes I drift off and forget what I'm supposed to be doing. I think someone else is . . .' And then he proceeded to count the other members of team. 'No . . . that can't be right . . .'

He looked genuinely distraught.

But just for about five seconds. Then he winked at Michael and said, 'We have autopilot.'

Michael was relieved . . . but not completely.

'Is there not, uhm, supposed to be someone watching it all the time, in case . . . you know . . . something goes wrong . . . ?'

'Yeah, pretty much.'

Bailey took another relaxing sip of his coffee.

'Uhm . . . shouldn't you . . . ?'

'If you're worried, take a look yourself, but I'm sure it's fine.'

Michael's mouth dropped open a little. 'You're serious?' Bailey nodded. 'I thought with all the trouble with terrorists, passengers weren't allowed in the cockpit any more – especially without the pilot, in the middle of the flight, in the middle of the ocean.'

Bailey set his coffee cup down and reached for the sugar. As he poured it in, he said, 'Kid, up here we make our own rules. Be my guest.'

It was *so* weird entering an empty cockpit lit only by the dozens of tiny lights on several instrument panels. The pilot's seat was vacant, as was the co-pilot's.

Ahead of him the night sky dotted with billions of stars, clearer than he had ever seen them. The clouds below were like a lush unbroken carpet of cotton wool.

Twenty-four hours before he had been marooned in a freezing-cold boarding school without a friend in the world, and now here he was more or less in sole command of a private jet, streaking across the Atlantic in pursuit of a missing satellite.

Michael could literally feel the adrenaline rushing through him.

He slipped into the pilot's seat. He knew this was an incredibly complex and sophisticated state-of-the-art aircraft worth tens of millions of pounds and also that he didn't know the first thing about how to fly it. But he desperately wanted to touch something. Push a button. It was almost as if he had a little devil on his shoulder urging him to do it. His hands hovered over the controls. They were millimetres away. He broke out in a cold sweat.

'Tempting, isn't it?'

Michael jumped. He glanced back at Bailey, standing in the doorway, coffee cup still in his hand.

'I wasn't going to—'

Bailey came forward and eased into the co-pilot's

chair. 'No feeling like it in the world. Here, let me just take the autopilot off . . . now, take a grip there, you fly her for a while.'

'*Seriously?*'

'Hell, why not, nobody up here but us chickens.'

'But what if—'

'What's the worst that could happen? Apart from you somehow causing a catastrophic loss of power, or making us flip over and lose control, or dropping thirty thousand feet like a stone, or exploding in midair? Nothing to worry about. There, she's all yours.'

'What . . . what do I do?'

'Just keep going straight ahead. She'll let you know if you're veering off course. Meantime, I'm going to catch forty winks.'

Bailey settled himself comfortably in his chair, clasped his hands in his lap, put his head back and closed his eyes.

Michael just looked at him. 'Are you . . . for real?'

One eye winked open. 'Partly. Only thing complicated about flyin', is taking off, and landing again. Apart from that, any idiot can do it. No offence.' He closed his eyes again. 'So take us to Canada, kiddo.'

Michael stared at the controls again and then out at the stars.

He wasn't sure if he'd *ever* been happier.

Chapter Nine

'Wind at seventeen miles per hour, visibility fifteen miles, light snow showers, temperature at minus fifteen degrees centigrade with a wind chill factor of minus twenty-five. Forecast for snow, snow, and afterwards, a little more snow. Ladies and gentlemen, we are now approaching Baring Island International. Fasten those seat belts.'

Bailey was back at the controls and Michael was in his seat at the rear. The Artists were busy checking their equipment prior to landing.

Katya had unceremoniously dumped a laptop on Michael an hour before.

'Bonsoir says you should familiarize yourself with where we're going.'

So he'd been trying to research Baring Island and its only settlement, Miller's Harbour, on the internet, but with Katya in the seat beside him studying her own laptop, he had found it difficult to concentrate. She was, he decided, even though she was doing nothing specific to annoy him, the most annoying person he had ever met. And he knew there was only one course of action open to him. He had to annoy her right back.

'Do you know that Baring Island is home to two-thirds of the world's population of lesser snow geese?'

Her eyes flicked up to him for a moment, and then back to her screen.

'And did you know also that three-quarters of the world's population of musk oxen roam the island?'

Her eyes remained fixed to her screen.

'And did you know—'

'Shut up.'

Michael nodded. Several times. '—that Miller's Harbour's population is only three hundred and twenty, most of them speak something called Inuvialuktun *and* English – thank God – and that nobody has the foggiest notion who the Miller in Miller's Harbour ever was?'

Katya closed her laptop, stood up and silently departed to another seat near the front.

Michael smiled, satisfied. He had flown a jet across the Atlantic and he was about to leap into action with the SOS Artists on an Arctic island teeming with caribou, musk oxen and polar bears, plus he had very successfully annoyed his mortal enemy. He was in a happy place.

Michael presumed Bailey was joking when he called it an *international* airport. It wasn't anything more than a worryingly short stretch of runway and a small brick building.

Two members of the Royal Canadian Mounted Police had driven out from the town to meet them and check their documents. As the Artists unloaded their gear Michael overheard a heated exchange between the police and Dr Kincaid during which the SOS founder was warned not to go hunting for the missing satellite – which, incidentally, they pointed out, wasn't missing at all – and Dr Kincaid said he had no intention of hunting for it, because he was just here on holiday with his family. His denial was somewhat weakened by a sudden clattering from above and the sight of a helicopter clearly emblazoned with the SOS logo coming in to land. It had been flown up in a staged journey from the organization's American base near Niagara Falls, and there were lots of slaps on the back and hand shaking when the crew emerged. The police didn't look happy at all, but there wasn't much they could do about it: there was just the two of them to cover hundreds of square miles of Arctic tundra. They drove off, warning that they'd be back once they'd spoken to headquarters.

A people carrier emerged from behind the terminal, and soon they were motoring down into Miller's Harbour, which gradually revealed itself as an odd, shapeless mix of permanent and temporary dwellings. They passed a health centre, several restaurants, a frozen harbour, advertising hoardings for guided tours to watch the polar bears, and the offices of Baring Oil, a small company Michael had read about on the internet. There was thought to be up to twelve billion barrels of oil and 63 *trillion* cubic feet of natural gas under the ice around the island, but local environmentalists had been campaigning to stop the oil companies drilling for it.

The Miller Hotel, the only one in town, had seen better days. There were just the two floors, and SOS had hired all but two of the rooms. They were using a small conference centre on the first floor as their base of operations, and as soon as he had helped them set up in there Michael buzzed about from table to table as search areas were determined, logistics calculated and local guides recruited, trying to pick up as much information as possible. When something was needed he made it his business to find out how he could get it. He felt great, part of the team. He was determined to make himself indispensable. He didn't even mind when Katya hissed at him, 'Enjoying being the gopher?'

'The what?'

'Go for this, go for that . . .' She smiled sarcastically.

Michael made a face. Maybe it wasn't that exciting *yet*, but it was still important. He didn't mind being a gopher. At least, not for now. He would show Katya and all of them what he was made of.

He was in the reception area, getting the Artists snacks from a machine, when he sensed someone behind him. He turned to find Mr Crown towering over him.

'Been looking for you, Monroe.'

'I was just—'

'Here.'

He thrust a khaki-coloured canvas bag into his hands. Despite the fact that Mr Crown was looking more menacing than ever, Michael couldn't help but smile. He was making it official – presenting him with his own Artists uniform. Michael greedily pulled at the zip and slipped his hand inside. He felt around for the black jacket with the SOS logo on the arm, the white T-shirt, the black trousers and boots, but there was nothing even remotely like that, only a small, hard rectangular object. Michael withdrew it and examined it warily. Was SOS so sophisticated that it had somehow shrunk his uniform to fit in such a handy plastic box?

'What . . . is . . . ?'

'Monroe – have you never seen a pencil case before?'

'Pen— yes, of course, but why . . . ?'

'Because you're going to school, that's why. There's a car outside waiting to take you.'

Mr Crown turned to walk away.

'What? *Wait.*' Michael's voice was a mix of anger and disappointment. Mr Crown turned slowly. 'What do you mean . . . school? You mean like . . . training, for SOS?'

'No, Monroe, I mean school. Miller High, I believe it's called. Now have a nice day.'

As he turned again, Michael snapped, 'No! I didn't come all this way to go to school!'

This time Mr Crown's eyes blazed – but when he spoke his words were as cold as the frozen air outside.

'And what do you think you *did* come all this way for?'

'To find the Eden satellite.'

'And how are you going to do that?'

'By . . . helping . . .'

Mr Crown poked one thick finger into Michael's chest. 'Listen to me. You're fourteen, and we're obliged to continue your education, so take the bag, shut your mouth, and get on with it.'

Mr Crown stormed away, passing Dr Faustus, who was leaning against the doorframe into the conference room with his arms folded. They exchanged the shortest of nods as he passed.

Dr Faustus smiled to himself, unfolded his arms and came across to Michael. 'Hey, relax,' he said.

But Michael was still shaking his head in disbelief. 'Why would he do that to me?' he snapped, still staring angrily after Mr Crown. 'Why would he bring me all the way out here just to send me to school?'

'*He* didn't. *We* did. And he's right, we still have to keep up your education. And it's also essential to the work we're doing here.'

Michael sighed. 'How exactly do you work that out?'

'Because it's part of the SOS ethos to interact with local communities. Usually they're the ones who know what's really going on, not the government, not the police, but the people who actually hack a living out of godforsaken places like this. So although it might not feel like it, you *are* working for us, Michael, you are doing something important.'

Michael hiked the bag up on to his shoulder. 'Well, it doesn't feel very important,' he said, before stomping down the stairs and out of the hotel.

The same people carrier was waiting outside. The driver was a local Inuit who introduced himself as Tommy G. Michael nodded at him and threw himself grumpily into the back. But instead of moving off, they sat for five full minutes without moving.

Michael was in no hurry, but eventually he said, 'Well, are we going or aren't we . . . ?'

At that moment the other back door opened and Katya climbed in, her face like thunder. She had an identical schoolbag. She secured her seat belt and stared ahead.

Michael opened his mouth to speak.

But she got there first.

'Don't say a word,' she growled.

Chapter Ten

Michael and Katya were just getting out of the vehicle outside the school when the SOS helicopter, taking advantage of a break in the weather, thundered by overhead at the start of its search for the Eden satellite. They watched as it grew smaller and smaller until finally it blended completely with the grey skies.

They turned to face the single pre-fabricated building that was Miller High.

'It's not a school, it's a shoebox,' was Michael's instant appraisal.

If Katya had an opinion, she kept it to herself.

A diminutive woman in a red puffa jacket and woollen hat appeared in the doorway, waved and stepped out into the snow.

'Michael? Katya?' She came towards them with one gloved hand extended. 'I'm Rachael, I'll be your teacher for the next few days.'

Katya shook her hand and smiled pleasantly.

Michael shook and did not.

Rachael said, 'We're small, we're very informal. I'm sure you have lots to tell us about your exciting life with SOS!'

As they followed her through the door Katya shot Michael an evil look and said, 'Be sure to tell them about life as a gopher.'

Michael shot back with, 'Be sure and tell them about . . .'

But didn't know how to finish it.

Luckily Katya was distracted by a sudden explosion of shouting and screaming. Rachael flung the inner door open to find that the pupils, who seemed to range in age from about six to sixteen, were all either out of their seats or standing on them roaring encouragement as two boys rolled around the floor wrestling and throwing punches at each other.

'Hit him, Cody! Hit him!' one of the girls was yelling.

'Kick his ass, Cody!' shouted one of the boys.

Cody, a big bruiser of a kid with a thick roll of fat around his stomach and a thin moustache on his upper lip, was pounding his fist into a younger-looking, slighter boy who already had a bloody nose and a split lip. But every time he got hit, he threw a punch back, and Cody's face was looking just as battered.

'Cody! Jordan!'

Rachael grabbed Cody by his sweatshirt and dragged him backwards. Jordan immediately leapt to his feet and hurled himself after Cody with such force that he would probably have knocked both his adversary and his teacher flying if Katya hadn't suddenly crouched down and thrown her shoulder into his chest, stopping him dead. Before he even realized what was happening she grabbed one of his arms, stepped inside it, and tossed him over her other shoulder.

Jordan landed with a *whump* on the damp floor.

Katya placed one foot on his chest to keep him in place and jabbed a warning finger at him. 'Stay,' she said.

Jordan glared at her, but made no further effort to move. When Katya looked around, everyone was staring at her.

Michael had to admit that the speed and strength and technique she had displayed were very impressive. And just a little bit scary.

But it was important not to let her think she was getting the upper hand. He clapped his hands and said,

'Well done, Katya! I have been training her in the art of self-defence, isn't she doing well?'

Now everybody was looking at him as if he was the boss.

All except for one.

As soon as Katya took her foot off him, Jordan jumped to his feet and stormed out of the classroom and out into the yard. Rachael yelled at him from the window to come back in, but he just kept walking.

'At least take your coat!' she shouted, but he paid no attention, and very soon he was swallowed up in the snow, which had begun to fall heavily again.

Katya said, 'Do you want me to go after him?'

'No, let him be.'

One of the girls shouted, 'His grandfather's a killer, that's why!'

Rachael clapped her hands angrily together. 'That's enough of that, young lady! Now back into your seats, all of you!'

There were nineteen of them, fifteen black-haired Inuit, the others the children of workers at Baring Oil. Rachael told Cody to go to the bathroom at the back to clean up his bloody face. He just shrugged and went to do it. Michael thought that was quite refreshing – at home in England there would have been a suspension, an inquiry; parents would have been called, social workers brought in to find out if there were problems at home. It would have been treated like a national crisis. Here they just seemed to get on with it.

When they had settled into their seats, Rachael finally introduced Michael and Katya, saying that they were here to learn all about life in Miller's Harbour, and in turn, she hoped they'd tell the class all about their exciting adventures with SOS.

Katya smiled at the class. 'Absolutely,' she said. 'I'll just hand you over to my friend Michael. He's had the most wonderful adventures with SOS, haven't you? Why don't you tell us all about your experiences with gophers?'

'No I really think—'

'Let's hear it for Michael!'

Katya led the applause.

He hated her.

He *really* hated her.

At the end of school, and with no sign of a taxi to pick them up, Katya told Rachael she was going back to the hotel to check in with the rest of the team. Michael knew that she was only telling Rachael so that she would not have to speak to him directly. He was as curious as she was to know how the search was progressing, but he let her walk on. He'd paid close attention to the route that Tommy G had driven that morning, and he was pretty sure she was walking in the wrong direction.

So she wasn't *that* smart.

Michael set off in the right direction and within ten minutes of trudging through the snow found himself . . . right back where he started. Rachael was just locking up the school. She smiled when she saw him and said, 'You look lost.'

'Just familiarizing myself with the layout of the town. Heading back to the hotel now.'

She nodded.

He set off.

'It's the other way!' Rachael called after him. 'You need to go north!'

'I know! I'm taking the scenic route.'

Fifteen minutes later, still lost, his toes numb with cold, Michael found himself outside a plain brick building with *Miller's Harbour Eskimo Museum* in switched-off neon above it. A poster promised a thousand pieces of Inuit sculpture, an interactive documentary on the history of the region and its people and a live recreation of life as it was in an Inuit village one hundred years ago.

It sounded like the most boring place on earth – but at least it would be warm.

Inside, the entrance hall was crammed with racks of T-shirts, posters and postcards sporting glossy pictures of polar bears and caribou. There were wildlife DVDs and CDs of traditional Eskimo songs. There were little statues of Eskimos fishing at holes in the ice, except the holes were ashtrays. He picked one up and it said *Made in China* on the back.

It was all *very* tacky.

There was a man sitting behind a desk, looking bored. Michael pointed towards a moth-eaten curtain that led to the museum proper.

'It's free, right?'

The man tapped a small cardboard box with a slit in the top. 'You make a donation.'

'How much is that?'

'Whatever you think is appropriate.' Michael began to pat his pockets. The man said, 'You donate at the end, once you've enjoyed the Eskimo Experience.'

Michael nodded. Then he said, 'Do you prefer Eskimo or Inuit?'

'Inuit.'

'Then why do you call it an Eskimo museum?'

'So that stupid tourists will understand what we are.'

'I'm not a tourist.'

The man shrugged.

Michael moved through the curtain.

He had called it correctly.

It *was* the most boring place on earth.

He knew he *should* learn as much as he could about the Inuit. But he wanted to be out *there* doing it, not in *here*. He had signed up with SOS for the adventure, not to look at something as ridiculous as the exhibit now in front of him: a real-life Inuit in seal skins, moving around a very cheap-looking recreation of an igloo, pretending to shoot at a mangy stuffed polar bear with a suspiciously plastic-looking bow and arrow.

It looked *pathetic*.

Michael couldn't help himself. He laughed out loud.

The Inuit turned to face him.

It was Jordan, his classmate of about twenty seconds. He had a swollen eye, and a thick lip, and there was blood hardened around his nostrils.

And he was looking every bit as angry as he was that morning.

'What're you laughing at?' he growled.

'Nothing.'

Michael turned away, still grinning. He couldn't help himself.

He tried to interest himself in the sculpture, the pottery, the ancient hunting weapons and the sepia-tinted photographs of early-twentieth-century Inuit life in Miller's Harbour, but it was boring, boring, boring. The documentary, which looked like the most interesting thing in the entire museum, was being shown on a touch-screen television. But he couldn't get the sound to work.

Michael gave it another ten minutes before deciding to head back to the hotel. At least his feet were warm again. He breezed back out into the reception area and headed towards the door. The man behind the desk looked up, cleared his throat and nodded pointedly at the donation box.

Michael kept walking.

The museum deserved precisely *nothing*. And besides, he had no money.

He emerged into a biting wind and renewed flurries of snow. He had only walked twenty metres when a voice behind him said, 'Hey!'

Michael turned . . . straight into a fist.

The blow knocked him on to his back. As he tried to get up, Jordan landed on him, pinning him to the sidewalk.

'You laughing at me?' the young Inuit furiously demanded.

But before Michael could unscramble his senses enough to respond, another punch cracked into the side of his face.

Chapter Eleven

It was Tommy G who pulled Jordan off and threw him back against the museum wall, cracking his head. As he reeled away, clutching the back of his skull, Tommy kicked him in the ass before turning to haul Michael up. He asked him if he was OK, and then blocked him as he tried to go after Jordan to punch his stupid face.

'Leave him, leave the damn stupid kid alone,' said Tommy G. He guided Michael into the people carrier, which had glided up unnoticed while they'd been fighting in the snow. 'They sent me to look for you.'

'They did?'

'Sure. The girl said you were lost. They're all worried.'

Oh *brilliant.*

'I wasn't lost, I was . . . exploring.'

Tommy G shrugged. He got in and started the engine. As they slid past the entrance to the museum,

Jordan yelled something at them in what Michael supposed was Inuit. Tommy slammed on the brakes and made as if to get out. Jordan quickly disappeared back through the door.

'That kid has a problem,' said Michael, rubbing at his sore jaw. 'He was fighting in school this morning, and he just attacked me there for no reason at all.'

'Yeah, he sure is screwed up. Runs in the family.'

'What do you mean? Oh – someone said at school his grandfather had killed someone . . . ?'

'That's what they say. Took some rich guy out hunting polar bear, guy never seen again.'

'Murdered him?'

'That's what they say. Got him in jail here, ranting and raving like a lunatic. Says bear the size of a house attacked them, tore the hunter to shreds, but left him alone because he prayed to the ancient spirits. I tell ya, I thought there was a bear as big as he says, I'm on the first plane outta here. Cops say he was drunk, they probably had a row over money, he killed the hunter and let the snow bury the evidence.'

'And what do you think?'

'I think he's a crazy old bird, that's what I think. That boy though, that boy Jordan, about the only one believes him. Old guy's never been off the island, but they're gonna transfer him soon to the proper jail on the mainland. Boy thinks his grandpa will die there, he'll never see him again. So yeah, he's pretty upset, he been throwin' punches at anyone who looks at him. Pity, he's a good kid, smart.'

'You seem to know a lot about him.'

'Yeah, well. He's my nephew.'

'Oh. Right. But wouldn't that make the old guy . . . ?'

'Sure. He's my dad. Don't mean he ain't a killer, though.'

In the few hours Michael had been gone from the Miller Hotel it had been transformed into a state of bedlam. Because the 'supposed' Eden crash on Baring Island was not putting any lives at risk – 'human' lives, at least – Dr Kincaid had chosen not to operate in secrecy, but to use the SOS presence in the Arctic to publicize the search for the missing satellite and his theory that it might have been shot down by those who didn't want the true extent of global warming to be exposed.

And if it was one thing Dr Kincaid was good at, it was publicity.

Dozens of camera crews, reporters, treasure hunters

and conspiracy theorists had descended on the town in general and the hotel in particular. And those were just the ones who were candid about their reasons for being there. There was also a sudden influx of secretive-looking people who might have worked for the Canadian government, the CIA or any number of foreign powers or huge multinational corporations with an interest in either finding the satellite themselves or destroying all evidence of it. But being secretive types, they weren't saying.

The car park at the back of the hotel had been transformed into a heliport. And it seemed like every local resident was outside selling their wares at exorbitant prices: hunters and guides were offering their services; bedrooms, snowmobiles, huskies, sledges, rifles, fur-trimmed parkas, mittens, goggles, boots, sleeping bags, tents, knives and binoculars were all on offer. One family had even set up a stall offering seal burgers.

Michael watched it all, fascinated. When he re-entered the hotel he made his way to the restaurant, where Dr Kincaid was holding a press conference. It was tightly packed and hot and sweaty under the TV lights. He spoke fluently and in useful sound bites about the search, the attempted cover-up and the threat to the local environment.

Bailey was standing with his arms folded by the doors at the back of the room.

'I take it this means you didn't find the Eden?' Michael asked.

Bailey answered without taking his eyes off his boss. 'Weather closed in again, barely got an hour out of it. Even getting back here was pretty touch and go.'

Michael tried not to show his relief. The longer they took, the longer he would have to prove that he was worth taking along to help. He knew it was selfish, but he couldn't help it.

'Problem is,' Bailey continued, 'all these guys – and there are probably many more on their way – they're all looking for the Eden as well. It's like a treasure hunt now. Most of them will have the right equipment; doesn't mean they know how to use it. If the Arctic decides to kill you, there isn't much you can do about it.' Bailey nodded across the restaurant. 'Notice anything about the camera crew in the middle, the reporter asking all the questions?'

Michael raised himself up on his tiptoes for a better look. There was a bald man with aviator glasses on a cord around his neck, demanding to know exactly what proof SOS had that the satellite had been shot down and accusing Kincaid of being deliberately vague in his answers.

'Apart from being obnoxious? No.'

'Keep looking.'

Michael studied the bald man some more – and then his cameraman and sound guy. Apart from the fact that they all seemed to be very well built, he couldn't see anything out of the ordinary about them. He looked around the other camera crews and reporters, comparing them. No, nothing seemed amiss, they were all just doing their work, asking questions, making sure their framing was right and that they recorded every word Kincaid uttered in order to analyse them all later.

But then he spotted it.

'Their camera isn't switched on. No red light, no monitor.'

Bailey nodded.

'But why would they . . . ?'

'Don't know. But interesting, no?' He unfolded his arms. 'I'm bushed, going for a lie down.' He started to turn away and then stopped. 'Oh – Mr Crown was looking for you.'

Michael's stomach turned over. Having Mr Crown looking for you could never be a good thing.

'What does he want?'

'Don't know – I was scared to ask.' Bailey winked and headed for the stairs.

Michael stood where he was, trying to decide what to do. His natural instinct was to avoid Mr Crown; but that was the story of his life to date, avoiding responsibility wherever he could, and where had that got him? A dozen different schools and a reputation as a troublemaker. He was trying to make a new start, trying to impress SOS enough to be included on their proper missions, not doing some kind of sad community work like going to school with the natives. He knew what he had to do. He had to step up and confront whatever it was head on.

Just as he turned to go to the logistics room in search of Mr Crown, Michael found his way blocked.

By Mr Crown.

'Trying to avoid me, Monroe?'

'No . . . I was just—'

'I hear you got lost out there.'

'No, I—'

'I'm told you got into a fight.'

'I was attacked and—'

'Do you know something, Monroe? We're not here to make enemies. SOS can't function properly if it can't relate to the local community. Little things snowball, and soon we're being chased out of town. So it's important to get on with people.'

'I didn't—'

'So here's what's happening. The boy you picked a fight with—'

'I didn't—'

'—his father, Dan Nappaaluk, has invited you for dinner, to make peace. A car is waiting for you outside. Remember, you're representing SOS, so be pleasant, don't do or say anything that's going to further ruin our reputation. OK?'

Mr Crown didn't wait to hear if it was OK. He just brushed past and entered the press conference. Michael stood in disbelief. How could Mr Crown have got it so completely wrong? He was on the verge of storming right back up to him to remonstrate when he saw the bald-headed journalist and his camera crew emerge and walk quickly towards the hotel doors. A moment later Mr Crown followed them out.

Michael waited until the doors had swung shut again before venturing after them. He emerged into the bitter cold just in time to see Mr Crown walking towards the car park but being quickly swallowed up by the swirling snow. His inclination was to follow, but he was distracted by lights flashing at him from the other side of the road. It was Tommy G and his people carrier. Michael sighed. He had been given his orders. Mr Crown and the mysterious camera crew would have to wait. He crossed over, nodding at Tommy as he passed the driver's window, then hauled open the side door.

Katya was sitting in the back, looking furious.

'You,' she snapped, 'are really messing up my life.'

Chapter Twelve

Jordan Nappaaluk was about as happy to see Michael and Katya as they were to see him.

That is, not a lot.

It was a small house, but modern and tidy. When they entered, Jordan's dad fixed Michael with a frosty look and said, 'I hope you'll be leaving a donation afterwards.'

It took several moments for him to realize that he'd already met Dan Nappaaluk behind the desk at the museum. And that he was only joking.

'They call me the curator down there, but really I mostly sell T-shirts. Still, it's work, isn't it, Jordan?'

Jordan grunted moodily.

As Michael, Katya and Jordan studiously avoided eye contact with each other, Dan gave a running commentary on the dinner preparations.

'When I was growing up everything we needed to eat was right outside our door. Seal and walrus mostly. Moose, caribou and reindeer when we could get it. Salmon, whitefish, tomcod, pike and char. Man, we smelled of fish all year round! We were healthy, though. You all want to try stinkfish? That's fish buried in seal bags in the tundra and left there to ferment. No? How 'bout muktuk? Jordan, you like muktuk, don't you? That's pickled whale skin and blubber. We eat it raw.'

Michael was feeling queasy.

Katya said, 'I'm happy with whatever you're making.'

'Well, sorry to disappoint,' Dan called from the kitchen, 'no muktuk tonight, but we're having something even more traditional. We having kayeffcee.'

Michael saw Katya's brow furrow.

'That's fine too,' she said.

She was sitting with her back to the kitchen door, so she couldn't see what Michael could now see, and it was all he could do to stop himself from bursting out laughing.

'You've had kayeffcee before, Katya?' Michael asked.

'No, but it's important to try new things.' She gave him a condescending look before lowering her voice and talking to him as if Jordan wasn't there. 'You know the typical Inuit diet is very high in fat, low in carbs, and you'd think they'd be very unhealthy, but they're not. Vitamin C, for example, is found in whale skin and in seal liver. Kayeffcee doesn't sound very appetizing, but it will undoubtedly be good for us. Although I'll bet you won't even try it.'

'How much?'

Before they could agree on a sum, Dan appeared with the kayeffcee and set it in the middle of the table.

It was contained in a red and white cardboard bucket; there was a drawing of an elderly man with a beard on the side together with the letters K, F and C.

'Yes, sorry to disappoint you folks,' Dan said. 'I don't much like eating traditional and Jordan just plain won't touch the stuff. Most nights we have Kentucky Fried Chicken. Buy a mountain of it on the mainland, freeze it. Yes, sir, Jordan loves his kayeffcee.'

Michael finally burst out laughing. So did Jordan. And, after a little, Katya joined in as well.

It was probably the only place in the entire Arctic circle where there was any thawing going on. Michael didn't exactly warm to Katya or Jordan, but they were talking, which was a significant improvement.

After they'd scoffed the chicken, Dan went off to do his own thing, leaving them in charge of a PlayStation

3. They played a skateboarding game between them, during which Jordan casually said sorry for punching Michael, and Katya said sorry for knocking Jordan over and standing on his chest; Michael looked at Katya and waited for her to apologize for being obnoxious, and she looked at him and waited for him to apologize for trying to muscle his way into SOS, but neither actually said anything.

Michael said, 'Sorry to hear about your granddad.'

'He didn't murder no one,' said Jordan, without moving his eyes from the screen.

'Tommy G said—'

'Tommy G doesn't know what the hell he's talking about!'

Jordan hurled the PS3 controller down and stalked out of the room.

Katya went after him, giving Michael a sarcastic, 'Well done,' as she passed.

Michael followed her outside to an enclosed yard, where Jordan was pacing back and forth. He started to say he was sorry, but Jordan cut him off.

'Not your fault,' he said. 'It's the police, it's my dad, it's Tommy G, it's everyone, not believing him. Used to be everyone listened to the old ones, now they hear something on the TV news and suddenly that's the truth. I know my grandfather. I know he didn't kill anyone. He's lucky to be alive. There's a bear out there, biggest bear in the world, and it killed the hunter, and it let my grandfather live because . . .' He hesitated for a moment. 'My grandfather is *angakkuq*.'

'He's what?'

'He's like a shaman,' said Katya. 'A spiritual leader.' Jordan nodded, pleased that Katya at least understood what he was saying. She looked pointedly at Michael. 'The Inuit have a very rich mythology. It happens when a people have a lot of time to kill, like waiting for the caribou to return, or seals to pop up at ice holes.'

'Or when they're out hunting kayeffcee.'

She made a face at him. Jordan didn't seem to notice.

'No one much believes any more,' he said, 'but my grandfather never changed. He says all living things can be controlled if you invoke the right spirits. He used to tell me stories about fantastic creatures and evil spirits, would scare me half to death, even though he didn't mean to. Because he said . . .' He glanced at both of them, then back at the snow. 'He said I had it too, that I could talk to spirits. He said I was *angakkuq*. I don't think I am, but he says one day I'll know. He says the bear that killed the hunter, he says it's the spirits showing us how unhappy they are with what's going on.'

'What's going on?' Michael asked.

Jordan shrugged. 'He has different words for it, but he's talking about the sea ice melting, the polar bears starving, the whole global warming thing, you know? And that's why the bear spared him, to warn everyone to stop what they're doing, to leave us alone. We have to go back to the old ways.'

'And is that what you believe too?' Katya asked.

'Yeah. Back to the old ways.' He grinned sheepishly. 'Though I would kind of like to hold on to the PlayStation.'

The door opened behind them and Dan looked out. 'What you kids doing out here? You'll freeze. Jordan, you ain't filling their heads with bull?'

'No Dad, that's your job.' Jordan scowled at his father and pushed past him into the house.

Dan shook his head after him. 'Sorry about that,' he said. 'And if he gave you that crap about controlling animals through spirits, well I tell you, he ain't too good at it, he's been bitten by dogs three times this year alone.'

From somewhere inside, Jordan shouted, 'Twice!'

'Anyway. Your lift's here.'

Michael and Katya thanked him for dinner. Jordan didn't come out to say goodbye. When they got into the people carrier they sat quietly in the back. They knew instinctively not to discuss what Jordan had said in front of his uncle. They would probably have got in to it as soon as they arrived back at the hotel, but all thoughts of it disappeared as soon as they saw the neon lights flashing outside it. There was a police car and an ambulance. A crowd had formed, with locals and TV crews alike jostling to get a better look.

Michael and Katya jumped out of the vehicle and squeezed their way to the front, just in time to see a stretcher being loaded into the ambulance.

Mr Crown was lying on it.

Dr Faustus was at his side, desperately trying to control the flow of blood from a gash in the side of his head.

Chapter Thirteen

'It was just an accident. He slipped on the ice. Nothing to worry about. We'll get him to hospital, get him stabilized. He'll be fine. No, there is no suggestion of foul play. There is a suggestion of extreme slippyness. He's a big guy, when he goes down, he goes down hard. Now if you don't mind, we're here for a reason. We need to get on with it.'

That was Dr Kincaid, addressing the assembled press, trying to be upbeat. But when he retreated from the bright television lights into the SOS HQ on the first floor Michael could read the concern on his face. Mr Crown was being airlifted to the nearest large hospital. Dr Faustus called from the helicopter and said he had slipped into a coma. The other Artists gathered together, discussing the situation in grave tones. Katya was part of the group, asking questions freely; Michael stood on the fringes, not sure if he should or could contribute, at least until he heard that Mr Crown had been found in the car park.

'I saw him,' Michael said.

Only Bailey heard him. 'What was that, Michael?'

They all turned to look at him.

'I saw Mr Crown going to the car park. He was following one of the camera crews.'

The Artists exchanged worried glances.

'Which crew, do you know?' Bonsoir asked.

Michael nodded at Bailey. 'You saw them. The ones who weren't filming.'

'You're sure?' Katya asked.

'No, I'm just making it up. *Yes*, I'm sure.'

'Did he say why he was following them, or what he was going to do?' Dr Kincaid asked.

Like he was going to tell me.

Michael shook his head. 'Sorry, I . . .'

'No,' said Dr Kincaid, 'well done, Michael. You're the only one who noticed. OK, folks, we're all upset by this, but let's be on our guard. There are people who want to stop what we're doing. We need to remember what we're up here for. Hard as it is to say, it's more important than any individual. We'll let the local cops know what we know, and let them handle it. Although from what I've seen of them I'm not expecting much. Bailey, can I have a word?'

Michael was sure he had the smallest room in the hotel. But he had absolutely no complaints at all. Small meant it was easier to keep the heat in. He got into bed and tried to sleep, but wild thoughts crowded into his head: the fight Mr Crown must have put up before he was overwhelmed by the fake camera crew; what must he have discovered about them, overheard or witnessed? Had he been ambushed? Had he tried to take on all three of them himself?

Michael had known that joining SOS was a passport to danger, but he had imagined that most of it would come courtesy of Mother Nature herself: hurricanes and floods and earthquakes and soldier ants and wild beasts. Not by way of a vicious assault by heavily muscled thugs. He wondered how long Mr Crown had lain in the subzero temperatures before he was discovered, his blood staining the virgin snow red. Michael shivered involuntarily, and not from the cold. Burying himself in the warmth of his blankets, he closed his eyes. There was a sudden banging on his door. He shook himself and rolled out of bed. When he opened it Katya was standing there. She raised an eyebrow.

'What?'

'*School?* Duh.'

She turned away. Utterly confused, Michael was about to shout something not very pleasant after her when he noticed that his watch was reading 8 a.m., and that there was a weak sunlight coming through the window.

It was morning *already*.

Five minutes later, barely showered and incompletely dressed, Michael stumbled outside to find Katya tapping her foot impatiently.

'I don't suppose I've time for break—'

'No.'

She started walking. Michael hurried after her.

'Where's Tommy G? Isn't he supposed to—'

'I told him we didn't need him today.'

'What? Why? It's *freezing*.'

He hadn't dried his hair properly. He could feel it solidifying.

'Because we're not going to school. At least, not directly.'

She marched on. Michael scuffed through the snow after her.

'Then where are we going?'

'Jail,' she said.

He drew level with her.

'Jail.'

'Did you not hear it last night?'

'Hear what?'

'The howling.' She stopped. 'You *slept* through the howling?'

'*What* howling?'

Katya rolled her eyes. 'You're really not cut out for this, are you? Nobody could sleep because of it. We were all out listening to it. It was coming from the jail.'

'You've lost me completely.'

They were just coming level with the police station now. Michael stepped towards it, but Katya kept straight ahead.

'Isn't the jail . . . ?'

'No. You idiot. Not the human jail.'

'Have aliens landed or something?'

'Polar bears, you numbskull. Didn't you read about the town at all? They have a polar bear jail!'

'Of course I read about it!' She was now leading him towards a large breeze-block building. 'That's it down there – it used to be a hospital.'

'A mortuary.'

'Right. Twenty years ago they turned it into a jail for bears who wandered into town looking for food and were reluctant to leave. Eventually they're taken back to the wild.'

'Thirty years ago. And because there's apparently not much food out there right now, it's packed full. And every last one of them was making such a racket last night the whole town was up. Except for you.'

'I was *tired*.'

But Katya wasn't listening. She'd spotted Jordan, standing in the middle of the road, staring at the jail.

His eyes didn't leave it as they stopped beside him.

'I guess you heard it last night,' said Katya. Jordan nodded. 'At least they've quietened down now.'

'They will start again soon.'

'How do you know?'

'Because my grandfather is sleeping now. But when he wakes he will call to them again, and they will answer.'

Katya nodded. Michael rolled his eyes.

'You coming to school?' he asked.

'No, sorry. Going to see my grandfather. Maybe later.'

'OK, see you later.'

Michael started to walk on. Katya hesitated.

'Anything we can do to help, Jordan?'

He shook his head. 'You folks concentrate on saving the planet.'

It was heavy with sarcasm. He turned and began to walk in the opposite direction.

'Jordan . . . that's not fair. If you need us to—'

He kept walking.

'Don't waste your breath,' Michael called back.

Katya watched for a few moments as Jordan tramped unhappily away, before hurrying after Michael. As she came up beside him he couldn't help but mimic the young Inuit.

'He will call to them again, and *they will answer*! What will they say, do you think? *There's a nutter who thinks he can talk to us*?'

Katya walked with her hands thrust into her pockets and her eyes down.

Michael laughed. 'You're not falling for all that spooky stuff?'

'It is part of the SOS ethos to treat traditional beliefs seriously.'

'It is part of the SOS ethos . . . man, you gotta lighten up. Not only has his granddad murdered someone, he's turned into Doctor Dolittle as well!'

They were just approaching the school when the

howling began again. The children playing outside stopped, and looked at the sky. Rachael appeared and began to usher them inside. When the last one entered the classroom, she stood in the doorway herself and looked up.

It was eerie.

It was spooky.

'It sounds like they're in pain,' said Michael.

'It sounds like they're calling for help,' said Katya.

Chapter Fourteen

Rachael did her best, but the younger ones were spooked and it was only when Katya took it upon herself to tell funny stories about her time with SOS that their attention was, albeit briefly, diverted from the ominous sounds emanating from the Miller's Harbour polar bear jail.

Michael quite enjoyed the stories himself, although he wouldn't tell Katya that in a million years.

Jordan didn't turn up. When they finished for the day Katya said she was going to look for him. Michael said he was going to look for him too. Katya said she said it first. Michael said he didn't care. They both shook their heads and started walking in the same direction.

'Stop following me,' said Katya.

'Stop following *me*,' said Michael.

They trudged to the police station first to see if he was still with his grandfather, but when they knocked on the door a frazzled-looking cop told them to get lost. He had enough on his plate. They called next at Jordan's house, but there was no one home. They were on their way back to the hotel when Michael said he was going to try the Eskimo Museum. Katya said that was where she intended to go.

'I thought of it first,' said Michael.

'Yeah, *right*,' said Katya.

Dan Nappaaluk was in his usual position, looking bored behind his desk, and he didn't brighten much when he saw his visitors.

'First of the day,' he said, 'and probably the last. Can I interest you in a T-shirt? Perfect weather for it.'

Michael said, 'We were looking for Jordan.'

'He not at school?'

'No,' said Katya.

'Yes,' said Michael.

Dan smiled. 'He's probably up feeding the dogs. My dad has a tour business, a one-man operation. With him in jail, there's no one to look after the animals.'

'I thought the dogs disappeared out where the . . . you know, murder thing happened,' said Michael.

'They did, but he has four teams for when it gets busy, in hunting season. Jordan helps him out. And now with everyone looking for some crazy rocket, school takes a back seat. Gotta earn money when we can up here. But it's hard. Most of them tourists, they want snowmobiles, think dogs are old news. Don't realize the snowmobiles only go so far, break down, run out of gas. Them dogs, you toss 'em some food once in a while, they keep going for ever. They may go slower, but they don't stop.'

'The tortoise and the hare,' said Michael.

'That's about it,' said Dan. 'Hired one team out late last night, already dark. Told them there was a storm coming in, but nothing would stop them. They knew the choppers would be grounded, thought it would give them an advantage finding that rocket.'

Michael and Katya exchanged glances.

'Wasn't a bald guy, two others?' Michael asked. 'Muscles out to here?'

Dan nodded. 'You know 'em?'

Michael nodded. 'Kind of. Say which direction they were going?'

'Nope.'

'Did you hire out guns to them as well?' Katya asked.

'Nope. Had their own.'

The door behind them opened and what appeared to be a genuine tourist entered the museum. Michael said they'd better be going. As they turned away Dan said, 'Forgetting something?'

Michael looked perplexed.

Dan nodded down at the cardboard box with the slit in top.

'Gotta make a living,' said Dan.

Michael patted his pockets helplessly. He still had no money.

Katya put a coin in.

Dan peered in after it. 'That,' he said, 'ain't gonna keep the wolves from the door. And up here, I mean that literally.'

The hotel lay between the Eskimo Museum and Paul Nappaaluk's home on the outskirts of town, so they called in to check if there had been any progress in the hunt for the Eden and on Mr Crown's condition, but there wasn't much news. Bailey was still out on the helicopter, but his regular reports back to HQ merely confirmed what they already suspected. The snow had successfully blotted out any residual heat left in the satellite, making it impossible for their thermal-imaging equipment to pick it out. They were now largely relying on spotting physical evidence – which again would probably be masked by the snow. They had sophisticated sensors on board which could identify indicators of pollution and physical trauma in the ground, but Bailey said it was still like looking for a needle in a haystack, at night, with sunglasses on.

The news about Mr Crown wasn't any better. The doctors were keeping him in a coma to give his body a chance to repair itself. He had a hairline fracture to his skull. Dr Faustus was remaining with him until his condition became clearer. The local police were keeping an open mind on what had happened to him, but with the influx of reporters and treasure hunters and adventurers into town, they simply didn't have the manpower to investigate properly.

As they were setting out to visit Jordan, Bonsoir zoomed up on a snowmobile. It had been hired locally and swiftly emblazoned with an SOS sticker.

'Don't suppose we can borrow that?' Michael asked.

Bonsoir shook his head. 'You have to be sixteen.'

Michael looked incredulous. 'I see kids of seven or eight on them round here!'

'I know,' said Bonsoir, getting out of the snowmobile, 'they're *very* naughty.'

He laughed and went to step up into the hotel. Katya moved to one side to let him pass; so did Bonsoir; they bumped into each other.

'Sorry,' said Katya.

'You're not safe to walk, let alone use a snowmobile,' said Bonsoir, and continued on inside.

Michael was itching to snap something cheeky after him, but he held his tongue. It wasn't his fight. Katya, he guessed, was just too chicken. She said nothing, just shook her head. But when she was sure he was gone she looked at Michael and smiled widely.

'What?' He was slightly unnerved by the very concept of Katya smiling.

Katya opened her hand. Bonsoir's snowmobile keys.

'You . . .'

'I did.'

Katya climbed on and inserted the key. As it started up she nodded at Michael. 'Coming?'

Michael got on behind her. 'Thanks,' he said.

'Don't worry about it. When we get back, I'm blaming you.'

* * *

The snowmobile engine wasn't loud enough to drown out the sounds of yelping and snarling as they approached Paul Nappaaluk's ramshackle house. They found Jordan out back, fastening a team of dogs into their harnesses and traces and attaching them to a heavily laden sledge. When they called his name Jordan looked startled – and nervous.

Michael nodded down at the sledge and noticed the rifle strapped to the side of it. 'Going somewhere?'

Jordan continued securing the huskies. When Michael went to pet one of them, he almost lost his hand.

'Jordan,' Katya said firmly. 'Where are you going?'

The boy straightened and looked from Katya to Michael before letting his gaze fall somewhere in between them.

'In two days, they're going to take my grandfather to prison on the mainland. He's never been off the island. He's an old man. If they take him away, he'll never come back. He ain't done nothing. Evidence is out there, I'm going to find it.'

'How're you going to find it if the police . . . ?' Katya asked.

'The police? They're from the city. They couldn't find . . . well, they don't know up here, that's for sure.

My grandfather takes hunters out every year, pretty much the same route. Sure, it snows and hides things, but if you know where to look, you know *how* to look, you'll find it. Everyone else thinks he's crazy. You hear all that howling? That ain't so crazy. It gives me a bad feeling.'

'Maybe that's the kayeffcee?'

Jordan squinted at Michael before smiling. 'Yeah. Maybe. But I have to do this.'

Katya moved closer to him. 'But you can't just . . . take off.'

'Why not? Because I'll miss school? Katya, my grandfather taught me how to live out there, his parents taught him, their parents taught them. We been surviving up here for a thousand years, ain't that big a deal.'

Jordan began to check his gear.

Katya shook her head and turned to Michael. 'We can't let him go.'

'You want to jump him?'

'It's not safe.'

'You heard him. He has one thousand years of knowledge. We've got what you read on the internet. I think he's in a better position to judge than we are.'

'It's still not right. He's upset about his grandfather, he's not in the right frame of mind.'

'Just you all keep talkin' about me like I'm not here.'

'What if you get lost, what if—?'

'Hey. I got the sun and stars to navigate by.' Jordan felt in the pockets of his parka and produced a small black device. 'And I got this. GPS. I'll be fine.'

'No.'

It was Michael saying no this time.

Jordan straightened. He seemed to be bigger than Michael remembered.

'You ain't gonna stop me.'

'No,' said Michael, 'I don't mean that. I mean – we're going with you.'

Katya's eyes shot towards him. '*What?*'

'We go with him. We help. Three have a better chance than one. Anything happens, accident or something, we help each other.'

'No,' Katya said firmly.

'I'm going by myself,' said Jordan.

'Katya, listen,' said Michael. 'You've all been drumming into me that part of being with SOS is about helping the local community. Well, one of them is about to be put in prison for something he didn't do. Or might not have done. Or might well have done, but if we can help prove it one way or another, then we should. We're here on Baring Island, at Miller's Harbour, with the SOS Artists, and we're doing exactly nothing to help anyone.' Michael paused. 'I didn't sign up to go to school every day and I'm sure you didn't either. This is our chance to contribute, to prove we can do something, to show we can use our initiative, that we're not scared, that we're capable of doing more than make coffee and track down mobile phone chargers. We should go with Jordan. He's from here, he knows this island like the back of his hand. We'll be perfectly safe. Let's do something, let's contribute. Katya, they'll hardly even notice we're gone.'

She was looking at him in a new light.

'That's a pretty passionate speech.' Michael shrugged. She looked at Jordan. 'What do you think?'

'Wouldn't mind the company.'

Katya took a deep breath. 'We can't just *go*. It would be irresponsible. They'll start looking for us, it'll distract them from the Eden hunt. Besides, we're not equipped, we can't just—'

'Everything we need is here,' said Michael. 'That right?'

Jordan nodded. 'My grandfather hires it out. We got plenty to spare.'

Katya dug one foot into the snow. 'We can't just disappear. And if we go and ask they'll say no. I know it. Besides, they're out on the search right now, they won't have time. If we wait until they get back maybe—'

'No,' said Jordan. 'If you're coming, come. My grandfather only has a little time left. I have to find what's out there, I have to go *now*.'

'God damn it!'

Dr Kincaid was in the midst of another interview and he didn't like being interrupted – or being seen to lose his temper. He apologized to the reporter before turning to Bonsoir, who was frantically gesticulating towards him from the other side of the makeshift SOS HQ on the first floor of the Miller Hotel. Dr Kincaid asked the camera crew to give him five and then hurried across.

'What is it?'

Bonsoir shook his head and showed him his mobile phone.

Kincaid read the text message with increasing incredulity. He looked up at the Artists' languages and logistics expert.

'They've gone out there . . . and they've sent a *text*?'

'Yes!'

'On some wild goose chase? Do they even know there's a blizzard coming in?'

'They say they're equipped, they say they're following the SOS ethos, and they say they need to prove that some old guy isn't guilty of murder.'

'God damn it!' Dr Kincaid exclaimed again. 'I should stop mentioning that ethos, it gets us into far too much trouble!' He sighed and sat on the edge of Bonsoir's desk. 'What do you think? If they have the right equipment? Katya's had survival training, right? It is helping the local community, right? It might actually do them some good, right? And they're in safe hands, right?'

Dr Kincaid was nodding, as if trying to convince himself.

And now he could see that Bonsoir was holding something back.

'OK,' said Dr Kincaid. 'Let's have it.'

'I called the boy's father.'

'He's not going to sue us, is he? Because that's all we—'

'No, sir. But he says Jordan, the boy, spends ninety-five per cent of his time on his PlayStation and that what he knows about surviving a blizzard you could write on the back of a stamp.'

'God damn it!'

Chapter Fifteen

They had two sledges with their supplies split between them. Each dog team had a leader dog at the front, steering the others and setting the pace. Directly behind them were the swing dogs, used to swing the others behind them around turns or curves as they changed direction. The wheel dogs were those closest to the sledge, generally calmer in temperament than the others, so that they wouldn't be unnerved by the sledge moving immediately behind them. In between the wheelers and the swing dogs were the remaining team dogs, the powerhouses providing the muscle to move them all relentlessly forward. The sledge driver stood at the back, with Jordan leading the way and Katya behind – she claimed to have worked with dogs while helping SOS rescue a team of Russian scientists marooned in the Antarctic, but Michael wasn't convinced. To him it looked like the dogs were making all the decisions and Katya was merely holding on for dear life. When it came to his turn to take control, he realized why. It was hard work.

Katya grinned back at him as he battled to impose his will. He wasn't sure whether she was grinning constantly, or her initial grin had just frozen into place. It was as cold as hell.

'I thought hell was warm!' Katya shouted back. 'And by the way, something frozen is hanging out of your nose. It's not very attractive.'

Michael wiped his sleeve carefully across his nose. He was worried it might break off.

From time to time Jordan stopped and studied his GPS, and then decided on a slight change in direction. With the sky thick with storm clouds, there was certainly no sun to guide them, nor would there be stars later.

Katya had a compass, but it was useless so close to the magnetic north pole. She had a GPS of her own on her mobile phone, which she studied from time to time before asking Jordan if he was certain they were going in the right direction. Jordan seemed sure, and as the local expert, she was happy to follow his lead, even if the path they were taking appeared confused; at one point she was even sure that they were heading back the way they'd come. Jordan himself wasn't happy with the progress they were making. Fresh snow made it more difficult for the sledges, and with one eye on the clouds above he urged them relentlessly forward until reluctantly deciding to make camp before the storm finally cut loose.

As the snow grew heavier and the wind picked up, Michael began to worry that they might not have time to pitch the tent properly, imagining that there were all kinds of ropes and poles that would have to be unloaded, organized and secured, but Jordan merely unfastened a clip and the tent sprang into shape all by itself. It took about three seconds. Then, as they stood admiring the simplicity of it, it blew away.

Jordan let out a yell, and Katya provided a shriek, as it tumbled away.

Michael did his best to control the dogs as they tried to join in the chase. The tent could have blown for miles across the featureless white plain if the wind hadn't suddenly changed direction and hurled it back towards them. Even then it was moving so quickly that it would have zipped past them again if Katya hadn't thrown herself on to it, thus reducing it from a glorified sail to a flat piece of material. She lay back on it to anchor it firmly and Jordan joined her to make sure. They were both laughing hysterically at the ridiculousness of it all.

But that didn't last for long.

The temperature was dropping by the minute and darkness was rapidly descending. They hurried back to Michael, tethered the dogs, secured the tent and crawled inside.

And what a relief it was, even to just get out of the wind.

Michael stripped off his mittens, his inner gloves, pushed up his face mask and tinted goggles and slipped off his Cabelas boots. As he massaged his frozen toes Katya broke out a small propane stove and began to melt snow, giving them a running commentary about how important it was to keep hydrated while simultaneously warning them against eating the snow as it was. It would just make them colder.

Jordan winked at Michael and produced a can of Coke.

Katya scoffed. 'It'll be frozen solid.'

Jordan popped the can and took a drink. He offered it to Michael. As he was taking a sip Katya said, 'How did you . . . ?'

'Easy. Kept it in the warmest place I could think of. My underpants.'

Michael spat out his mouthful.

Katya shook her head and held up a tin of food from the supplies Jordan had brought. 'There's nothing but franks and beans here.'

'I like franks and beans,' said Jordan. 'I was only planning for myself, until you two hitched a ride.'

'I like franks and beans too,' said Michael.

'But it's all there is! What kind of a balanced . . .' She sighed. 'I don't appear to have any choice. But at this rate we'll be farting our way across the Arctic.'

And that got them all laughing.

The tent was rattling madly in the fifty knot winds. It was twenty below zero, and when Michael peeked outside the snow was falling so heavily that the dogs were already buried under it.

'Won't they . . . suffocate?'

'They can sleep under it fine,' said Jordan. 'If it becomes too heavy on their traces they won't be able to free themselves, so every few hours, one of us needs to go dig them out.'

'Sooner or later,' Michael said, 'I'm going to need a pee.'

'Well, you do it then. But if you go out in that,' said Katya, 'your thing will freeze up and drop off.'

'My . . . oh. Right. In that case, I'd be better doing it in here.'

'Ew-yuk.'

'I'll probably need a number two as well,' said Michael.

'Me too,' said Jordan, 'though we don't call it number two. We use an old Inuit word.' He nodded at Katya. 'You may not be able to pronounce it.'

'I can manage most languages,' said Katya. 'Try me.'

'OK, repeat after me: Inee . . .'

'Inee . . .'

'Da*dump* . . .'

'Dadump . . .'

'No, it's da*dump* . . .'

'Da*dump* . . .'

'Better. Now repeat: Inee . . .'

'Inee . . .'

'. . . da*dump* . . .'

'. . . da*dump* . . .'

'That's it – now run them both together . . .'

'Inee . . . da*dump* . . .'

'Again . . .'

'I nee . . . da*dump* . . .'

'Again . . .'

'I nee . . . da*dump* . . .'

'Well, if you need a dump that badly, you better go outside.'

Michael had almost passed out from holding his laughter in for so long. Katya's eyes blazed.

'Oh . . . you . . . you . . . you . . . *boys*!'

Michael and Jordan were rolling around in hysterics. They could barely speak. When Michael did manage to get some words out he only added fuel to the fire by suggesting that after her dump she might fancy some *kayeffcee*.

Katya hurled cold beans at him.

Michael threw them back.

Jordan shouted, 'Food fight!' and joined in.

A couple of days before he'd been complaining about the cold while stuck in his miserable boarding school back in England. Now here he was, camping in the middle of a blizzard, with frozen beans stuck in his hair, the wind howling outside, a muffled yelping coming from the dogs, and a *tsk-tsk-tsk* beat coming from inside Jordan's sleeping bag, which he had zipped up over his head so that he could better concentrate on his PSP. It was pitch black.

'You awake?' Michael asked.

'I am now,' said Katya.

'I was just thinking how surreal this all is.'

'You get used to it.'

'How many other . . . missions, adventures, whatever you want to call *this* . . . have you been on?'

There was a long pause, and at first Michael didn't think Katya was going to answer. But eventually she said, 'Three.'

She waited for him to snigger, or to say something smart. When it wasn't forthcoming she said, 'Well, technically, two.'

He was quiet for another few moments, then he said, 'Lucky you.'

'I guess.'

'How'd you come to join SOS?'

'My parents were killed during the—' She stopped suddenly. 'Did you hear that?'

'Hear what?'

'Listen.'

Michael strained to identify something different in the cacophony that was already assailing them: the wind, the rattle of the tent, the yelping of the dogs, Jordan's PSP, a regular series of farts.

'I don't—'

'Wolves.'

And that was enough to cause a different kind of a chill to course through him.

Chapter Sixteen

The morning did not bring any respite in the weather. If anything the wind was stronger, the temperature lower, the snow harder. It didn't need to be said that they weren't going anywhere. As Jordan fired up the stove again and heated yet more beans for breakfast, Michael asked Katya if she'd heard anything from SOS.

'Sure, got a text. They said to be careful, storm could last a couple of days.'

'What about Mr Crown?'

'Nothing.'

But there was something about the way she hesitated when answering, without looking up, that made him think she was holding back. He had briefly had the same thought last night when she suddenly claimed to have heard wolves. He certainly hadn't; when he tried to get her back to talking about how she'd come to join SOS there'd been no response, and he presumed she'd fallen asleep. But maybe she just didn't want to say. He had to remind himself that although there had been a certain thaw in their relationship, they weren't friends, and they remained rivals. She still resented him being with SOS and might yet sabotage his efforts to become a full member of the team.

They ate in silence. When they were finished they scooped in snow to help clean the dishes. Jordan struggled against the wind as he crossed to dig out the dogs' traces and then began to feed them, which was a signal for pandemonium to break out. Each dog was due to get one and a half pounds of pemmican, a beefy mix of protein and fat, but Jordan had to kick out all around him so that he could dish it out evenly. It wasn't cruel, it had to be done. They could not only injure themselves fighting; if they got overexcited they could easily pull up their pickets from the snow and then there was a danger of them getting lost.

As they watched Jordan at work through the thick curtain of snow, Michael said, 'So you want to tell me what else was in that text?'

Katya's eyes remained steady on the feeding frenzy. 'Not particularly.'

'Look, Katya, we're stuck in a blizzard, in the middle of God knows where. We have to be able to trust each other.'

'Why?'

'Because if you fall down and break both your legs, you're going to expect me to get you home.'

Katya snorted. 'If you fall down and break both your legs, I'm leaving you.'

'Well, I'm sure Jordan will get me home.'

She snorted again. Then her eyes flitted up to him. 'That's what the text was about.'

'What to do if we break our legs?'

'Jordan. It reluctantly gave us permission to continue, but for us to check in regularly, and pointed out that according to his father Jordan has no experience at all of living in the wild.'

Jordan, as if sensing that he was being talked about, glanced across and gave them the thumbs-up. Michael did the same back.

'I was kind of thinking the Coke and the franks and beans were a bit odd. More like an armchair warrior than an ancient hunter. So what're we doing letting him lead us around? If we get lost out here, we're done for.'

'No, we're fine, I've been keeping track on my

own GPS. I'm just kind of curious as to where he's taking us. There's no discernible pattern, yet it doesn't feel random.'

'Well, maybe his grandfather's hunting trips didn't have a pattern. I mean, they were following wild animals . . .'

'Sure, but within that, I'm sure there are certain areas he would have taken the hunters to where he would have been pretty confident of finding bears. It just concerns me what Jordan expects to find.'

'Evidence that the hunter wasn't murdered.'

'You don't think it'll be buried under all this snow?'

'Maybe it is. Or maybe it *was*, so the police couldn't find it – but this blizzard is blowing so hard maybe it'll get exposed again?'

Before Katya could respond Jordan came hurrying towards them. He threw himself into the tent and then his sleeping bag, pulling it up around him. His teeth were chattering.

'Cold?' Michael asked.

There was nothing to do but wait for the weather to lift. Katya's mobile phone signal was intermittent, and Jordan's PSP soon ran out of charge, but they had brought extra fuel for the stove, and there was still plenty of food. Although it was freezing cold outside, within the tent the temperature wasn't too bad. They kept warm, they kept hydrated, and they waited.

But they were bored. The hours dragged by. Almost in desperation, as darkness began to fall again, Katya asked Jordan to tell them some old Inuit stories, and he kept refusing.

'I'd rather talk about ice hockey,' he said, 'or baseball.'

Michael wasn't the slightest bit interested in Inuit myths and legends, but he still thought they might be very slightly more gripping than stories about sports he had no intention of ever playing. He joined in Katya's campaign until eventually Jordan gave in.

So wrapped up in their warmest clothes, and safely zipped into their sleeping bags, Jordan asked them if they wanted to hear the tale of Sun Sister and Moon Brother, about how the sun and moon were created; or the story of Anarteq, about a boy who becomes a salmon, or of Angutisugsuk, the story of a family bewitched into fighting each other; or of the Inuit man who married a fox, or of the Inuit woman who adopted a polar bear, or . . .

Michael asked Jordan if he had any stories that didn't sound like . . . well, *crap* was the word he used.

'Michael, don't be so—' Katya began.

'What about the boy with enormous nostrils?' Jordan cut in.

'Now *that* sounds like a story.'

'It sounds made up,' said Katya, worried that this was another wind-up, like the *kayeffcee*.

'Of course it is,' said Michael. 'They're all made up! That's what myths and legends are! Stories handed down, usually to illustrate a point, that right, Jordan?'

'Absolutely. You want to hear it or not?' He took their silence as a yes. 'OK, so it's about this kid called Kautyayuq, right? He was out fishing on the sea ice, but it started to break up, and the piece he was on floated further and further away from his home, and he couldn't get back. Eventually it brought him to another settlement, and he was taken in by the people there, but they were real mean to him. He wasn't allowed inside the house, but had to sit in the doorway, and at night he had to sleep with the dogs. Whenever it was time to be fed, two big women would stick their fingers in his nostrils and drag his head inside. It wasn't even good food, but walrus skin. This went on for so long that his nostrils became enormous, and the people made a horrible game out of it, dragging him around the village by his nostrils, just for fun. But one night the people heard three polar bears prowling around the village and decided that this would be a good opportunity to get rid of Kautyayuq . . .'

'Kutya . . . ?' Michael asked.

'That was his name.'

'Sounds like Katya.'

'It does not, loser.'

'Listen. They forced Kautyayuq outside, certain that he would be eaten. But when they threw him out, the Moon Man came down from the sky and—'

'The Moon Man?'

'Yes, the Moon Man.'

'I was taking it seriously there, nostrils and all, but the Moon Man—'

'Will you just listen, Michael!' Katya snapped.

'Sure. To the Moon Man.'

'OK, the Moon Man came down and began to beat Kautyayuq – but it wasn't a cruel beating, what he was doing was beating all the weakness out of him. When he was finished, Kautyayuq began to grow bigger and stronger, and soon he was so huge that he was able to kill all three bears using only his bare hands. And then he went on the rampage and killed everyone in the village. Everyone except the two women who had been mean to him. He kept them alive so that he could drag them around the village by *their* nostrils.'

Jordan, who had been propped up on one elbow as he told his story, now lay back.

'Is that *it*?' Michael asked.

'Yup,' said Jordan.

'I was expecting something cheerful, or exciting, or . . . but that's just . . . nuts.'

'It was very, uhm, informative,' said Katya. 'But what is the moral of this story, or is there a lesson to be learnt from it – maybe in how it applies to the modern Inuit experience?'

Jordan nodded wisely for at least five seconds. 'What we learn from this story,' he said rather sagely, 'is that ice hockey and baseball are *much* more interesting.' He winked across at Michael.

Jordan was, Michael decided, really rather good at winding Katya up.

Chapter Seventeen

Michael knew something was wrong as soon as he opened his eyes. It wasn't that the wind had dropped for the first time in twenty-four hours, or the brightness that illuminated the inside of the tent, which meant that the snow had stopped and the sun was out. Those were indisputably *good* things.

It was the quiet.

The total and utter silence.

It was unnerving.

He glanced around him: Jordan and Katya were already up and out. He might just have rolled over and let them get on with whatever they were doing, but again, it didn't feel right. The dogs barking had been a near-constant irritant, even through the worst of the blizzard. Now they were silent.

It just *wasn't right*.

Michael slipped out of his sleeping bag and zipped up his jacket. He'd slept with his boots on. When he poked his head out of the flap he saw that Katya was standing about ten metres in front of him, binoculars raised. Michael quickly scanned the camp: no sign of Jordan, no dogs, one sledge missing. He hurried up beside her.

'Where's he gone?'

'Don't know. We had an argument in the middle of the night. When I woke up, he'd skipped town.'

'Argument? I didn't hear—'

'You were snoring. And he was as well – that's why I decided to take a look at his GPS.'

'You—'

'I told you I was worried about where he was taking us, the fact that there was no pattern to it. Well, I found out why . . .' She scanned the horizon again, then lowered the glasses and looked at Michael. 'We haven't been following his grandfather's hunting route. We've been following the polar bear that attacked them.'

'We *what*?'

'He admitted it. After a lot of shouting. Meanwhile, you were still snoring. I'm not sure you're cut out for SOS at all.'

'Just tell me what—'

‘Seems the old man was telling the truth. The polar bear attacked them and killed the hunter. His grandfather managed to escape, probably because the bear was busy eating his client. In the process it also managed to swallow the tracking device he was wearing.’

‘*Seriously?*’

‘No, I’m making it up. Yes, seriously. The grandfather insisted on all of his clients wearing them, because he reckoned most of them were stupid and were liable, despite his best efforts, to wander off or get lost.’

‘So we’ve been on a bear hunt and didn’t know it. A bear that now clearly has a taste for human flesh.’

‘Yep. But nothing to worry about. Apart from the fact that Jordan’s gone off with the rifle.’

‘And all the dogs with which to follow him or get home with.’

Katya nodded.

‘Why would he do that? I understand him taking off, but leaving us stranded?’

‘Because he was angry at being discovered. When I found out what he was doing he still wanted us to continue, but I told him no, we were going back to Miller’s Harbour, it was too dangerous. He tried arguing with me, but I wasn’t budging. You would have heard all this if you hadn't been snoring.'

'It's not my fault I snore.'

'Forget it. We better get something to eat, then strike camp and try to make our way back to base.'

'And just let him go?'

'We have no choice. He has the dogs, and we have no protection against bears or wolves.'

'And he knows nothing about surviving out there.'

'He has a spare tent, he has transport, he has food and he's armed. *He'll* be fine. We, on the other hand, will have to walk out of here. Without the dogs it's going to take us two days at least.'

'Then call Bailey. He can come and pick us up.'

'I probably would, if I had a phone. Jordan took it while I was sleeping. I guess he knew I'd call in back-up and stop him getting very far.'

'That means if they're tracking us from HQ, it'll look like we're still on the move? And going in a completely different direction?'

'Uhuh.'

'Bloody hell. Thanks a lot, Jordan. Thanks-a-bloody lot!'

Katya let out a sigh. 'Look, there's nothing we can do about it now. Let's just get started back. The weather's fine now, but it could close in again at any time.'

She turned back towards the tent, but Michael stood where he was. He surveyed the flat white plain, his eyes straining to pick out anything unusual, but it was like looking at a clean sheet of paper. He kicked at the snow in annoyance. He didn't know who was upsetting him more: Jordan for abandoning them, or Katya for abandoning Jordan. Yes, he knew the sensible thing to do was to get back to headquarters. It had been more than adequately drummed into him exactly how dangerous it was out here, and he knew how stupid and selfish Jordan was – not only going off alone, but also leaving them unprotected. Yet he couldn't shake the feeling that they were choosing the wrong course. They'd come out here for a reason, and they should see it through by whatever means they could. They shouldn't leave Jordan to his fate or run back to base like scared children – they should go after him.

'Will you give me a hand, *please*?'

As Michael was about to shout something back at Katya about not being so impatient, the snow under his foot suddenly gave way.

A snarling jaw and a set of jagged teeth snapped out at him.

Michael staggered back in shock and fell on to his backside.

Similar sets of teeth erupted from the ground in a semi-circle around him followed by an explosion of snow, like geysers going off in tight rotation. For several sickeningly shocking moments Michael was convinced that he had accidentally uncovered some previously unknown Arctic monster – until, the white coating falling properly away from them, he recognized their team of dogs, buried overnight by the blizzard and quite happy to sleep until disturbed.

The relief flooded through him. As the pack yelped hungrily Katya came hurrying across with their food, distracting them before they took a proper bite out of him.

As they leapt upon it in a frenzy, he couldn't help but grin at her.

'This changes things,' he said.

'I know. It'll cut the time back to base by two-thirds.'

'I mean, now we can catch him up, bring him home before he gets himself into trouble.'

'The quicker we get back to base, the quicker we get a rescue team out to pick him up.'

'No, Katya. When we set off from Miller's Harbour it was because we wanted to prove to SOS what we could do. Nothing has changed.'

'Everything has changed. Then we were just looking for evidence. Then we had a rifle, a means to protect ourselves, we had a GPS and a mobile phone. Now we don't have anything. It'll be hard enough finding our way back to town without getting lost, let alone exposing ourselves to any more danger.'

'Then if Jordan has the gun, and the GPS, and the phone, then it makes more sense we go after him. He only has a couple of hours' start, and it hasn't been snowing – we can easily pick up his tracks. Let's not go back crying for help.'

'I'm not crying. I'm doing the sensible, logical thing. It's what we're trained to do. If that polar bear did eat the hunter then it's not going to say no to us. We might not catch up with Jordan and his gun for days, and the bear might find us long before that. Michael, we need back-up.'

'We need to get Jordan.'

'No.'

They glared at each other.

'You'd leave him out there?'

'He has a gun and a map and we have neither.'

'Which is why—'

'No. I'm in charge here. You do as I say.'

'Who says you're in charge?'

'I am the senior member of SOS, I've done survival training, I know what I'm talking about. Now get the dogs and—'

'No. You might have done the training, and you may have been with them longer than I have, but I'm not leaving him out there.'

'That's just childish. We're going back to base. And for all we know, he'll be back there waiting for us. We are not going to run around out here like headless chickens.'

'Yes we are. Although not like headless chickens.'

'Don't make me make you, Michael.'

'*Make* me? You?'

'Yes. Me. If I want to, I can break you in half.'

'You and whose army?'

'Michael, I'm warning you.'

They glared some more.

'OK, then,' Michael said.

'OK, then, what?'

'We fight it out. If you win, we go back. If I win, we go after Jordan.'

Katya's eyes narrowed. 'That's not fair,' she said.

'Why? Because I'm bigger and stronger?'

'No, because you couldn't fight your way out of a paper bag.'

'Well, let's see.'

They began to circle each other.

Michael said, 'How do we judge who the winner is? First to draw blood?'

He made as if to rush her, and she jumped back.

'Blood, out here? How stupid are you? Polar bears can smell blood at twenty miles.'

'You just made that up.'

'Maybe. First to knock the other down, and keep them there for ten seconds.'

She made a feint towards him. He jumped back.

'Fair enough,' said Michael.

He rushed her.

She rushed him.

They collided, and each felt a surprising strength in the other.

Katya rocked back, Michael too.

She had her arms out in front of her now, hands open, ready to chop, but deliberately rotating them to make them the focus of his attention. He was mesmerized, knowing that any second one would snap out towards him. He knew she was trained in the martial arts. But he also knew what she couldn't have known: that he had trained in them as well. It was useful to be able to defend yourself when you moved school so often, when you were always the new boy, always the one the bullies tried to pick on.

Katya's foot shot out, catching him around the ear and knocking him sideways.

As he hit the ground, his head ringing, Michael kept rolling.

Katya dived after him. She landed on the soft snow where he'd fallen a fraction of a second too late. Michael sprang back to his feet just as Katya regained her own.

'Lucky shot,' he said.

'We'll see,' she replied, bouncing confidently up and down on the balls of her feet.

Now Michael held his own arms up, hands open, and began to rotate them, but in such a way that it looked as if he didn't know what he was doing, that he was trying to copy her but failing miserably. He could tell it was working by the faint smile that appeared on her lips. She moved forward, overconfident, but this time it wasn't a leg that shot out as she expected, but his right hand, and it caught her palm open on the side of her ear, and the force of it knocked her flying and for several long moments she couldn't hear *anything*.

Michael had the briefest glimpse of shock in her eyes as she went down, and this time he didn't make the mistake of waiting for her to land: he had her pinned to the ground before she could even begin to gather her senses.

'One,' he counted, 'two, three—'

—she bucked under him and before he could stop himself he was sailing through the air.

She was back on her feet and charging at him before he even landed. But he twisted as he fell, landing on his back, so that as she threw herself on him again he was ready. His feet caught her in the chest and used her forward momentum to throw her up and over his head. He rolled again and was back on his feet.

And so was she.

They looked at each other furiously, their breath freezing on their lips and nostrils.

Around them the dogs were going mad with excitement.

Michael moved forward. Katya backed away.

Then she moved forward, and he stepped back.

It was a dangerous dance.

They each inched imperceptibly closer, searching for an opening, a hesitation, a blink, poised to strike.

They didn't even think about the ridiculousness of it, fighting each other while lost in the middle of the Arctic, when they were supposed to be a team, when they were supposed to be representing SOS rather than trying to establish dominance over each other.

But they couldn't help it. They were just in the moment. The rest of the world might not even have existed.

Except suddenly, it *did*.

A gunshot rang out.

Katya knew enough to throw herself to the ground.

Michael stood there, looking all around him.

Katya's foot snaked out and knocked his legs from under him.

He hit the ground with a *whump* and she threw herself on top of him.

'Keep *down*!' she hissed.

And he saw the sense of it and didn't resist.

A second shot.

Katya scanned in every direction.

Nothing.

'It's not aimed at us. There's no cover to suck up the sound, it can travel for miles.'

'It's Jordan, then. He's found the bear. That settles it, we have to go after him.'

Katya nodded.

She was about to roll off him, but then she hesitated, and a smile slipped on to her face.

'One, two, three, four, five, six, seven, eight,

nine . . . and *ten* . . .' She winked. 'Which means I'm the winner.'

She was back on her feet before he said, 'That wasn't fair, you—'

'—you were beaten fair and square, loser! Now shut up and let's get going. Jordan's not shooting at squirrels!'

Chapter Eighteen

They circled the camp until they picked up Jordan's tracks and then set off at speed in a north-easterly direction. After almost five kilometres Katya stopped the dogs and pointed. Michael stepped off the sledge and together they moved across to examine a different set of tracks and dog prints coming in at an angle from the left to join with Jordan's.

Katya ran her fingers along the grooves cut in the snow. 'The impressions are identical to Jordan's and ours. Same make of sledge?'

'You're thinking, what if it's the fake camera crew? They hired their sledge from Jordan's dad, so it would be the same make.'

'It's possible.'

'Be a big coincidence, bumping into them out here. Besides, sledge runners are probably all pretty standard in size. And with the weather so bad, the aerial search for the Eden is going to be grounded, so there's bound to be dozens of sledges out looking for it – you saw what it was like in town, every Inuit and his granny was renting out their sledges. Most likely some idiot treasure hunter has got himself lost and is just latching on to the first set of tracks he finds.'

Katya nodded, but looked unconvinced.

'I don't like those gunshots,' she said.

'But we keep on, right?'

'Right. Let's just be careful.'

But it was impossible to be careful. They were on a flat, featureless plain, and the barking of the dogs carried just as far as the gunshots had. All they could do was follow the tracks and see where they led. If there was trouble ahead, the best they could hope for was that they would see it before it saw them.

And twenty minutes later, they did.

A black smudge on the horizon.

And then a second and a third.

Moving.

Michael was now guiding the sledge, so it was Katya who whipped out the binoculars and focused in.

'Wolves,' she said. 'Six . . . no, seven. Eight.'

'Just wolves wandering about, or . . .'

'They seem to be following the same course we are.'

'Which means?'

'They're curious. Or they're hungry.'

'You mean food scraps?'

'Maybe.'

'But maybe not? I thought wolves attacking people was just . . . a myth.'

'It's unusual, but not unheard of. Mostly women and children, but there was a hunter killed on the mainland a couple of years back. I was reading up on them – if they're hungry enough they'll attack anything. Or if they have rabies. Or even if they're teaching their cubs to hunt. With the blizzard, they're bound to be hungry.'

'Maybe the gunshots were to scare them off?'

'Could be.'

'So what do we do?'

'We press on.'

'No problem. We follow the wolves, the wolves follow the fake camera crew, the fake camera crew follows Jordan, and Jordan follows the man-eating polar bear. Do you think we're mad?'

'Probably. No . . . *definitely*.'

On they went, the wolves always on the horizon,

neither gaining ground on them nor losing them, thankful just to be downwind so that they weren't alerted to their presence.

As the morning slipped away a light mist began to gather, which made the wolves harder to pick out. Over the course of an hour this thickened into a freezing fog which blocked out whatever thin vestiges of sunlight there had been. Very soon they were straining to pick out the sledge tracks they were following and their pace inevitably slowed as a result. Boy, girl and dogs alike became increasingly jumpy. In fact, Michael could no longer see the lead dog.

Finally they came to a dead stop.

'I've lost the tracks,' said Katya. 'I had them . . . and then . . . they were gone. I think we've veered off course.'

It was as if they'd been dropped into a different world, a place where nothing moved, where every sound was swallowed up. There was no forwards or backwards, up or down. Even the dogs fell silent.

'Don't like this,' said Michael.

Eerie.

'It could lift in ten minutes,' said Katya, 'or we could be here for days. If we don't find the tracks again we're going to lose them. Jordan has GPS, he'll follow the bear. The fake camera crew will have GPS as well. They might be following Jordan or they might just keep going straight. Even the wolves have their sense of smell, they'll follow dinner.'

'Then we're just going to have to pick them up and keep going. Did Jordan leave the torch?'

'Think so. Hold on.'

Katya delved into the waterproof bag strapped to the side of the sledge, and quickly produced the torch. She flicked it on before handing it to Michael.

'OK,' he said, 'I'll walk with the lead dog, try and pick out the trail. It'll be slow going, but it's better than nothing.'

'Sorry,' said Katya, 'I just lost concentration.'

'Don't worry about it. At least it proves you're semi-human.'

'Which is more than you.'

But they both managed grim smiles.

Katya re-took her position at the back of the sledge.

Michael moved to the front. 'C'mon, fella,' he said, reaching for the leader's traces, 'nothing to be afraid of.'

In response the dog nearly took his hand off.

Michael quickly repeated to himself: *they're not pets.*

Luckily he had thick gloves. He gave the leader a cuff

around the head which quickly settled him, then took a firm hold of the traces. He shone the torch down and around. It took about ten minutes of slowly feeling his way to pick up the track again; they were about twenty metres off it – not much, but over the course of several hours it would have taken them miles in the wrong direction.

'OK,' he called to Katya, 'we're back in business.'

Katya urged the team forward, in the process jolting the sledge's runners out of the grooves they'd already begun to freeze into.

But their progress remained painfully slow. Michael had to walk hunched down, trying to keep the beam steady on the vague outlines the two sledges had left in the snow. The dogs seemed particularly anxious in the fog and it took much of his strength to stop them from breaking into a charge that might take them out of it.

Another half an hour passed in that netherworld. Michael guessed they hadn't travelled much more than a kilometre and a half. He paused for a moment, straightened his aching back, then raised the torch and aimed the beam into the fog bank, hoping for some sign that it was lifting or at least lightening – and was startled to see two sets of yellowy eyes reflecting back at him.

Michael was so shocked that he dropped the torch.

As he scrambled to retrieve it the lead dog gave a low growl and cowered down, and the others followed suit.

'What is it?' Katya called as the sledge came to an unexpected halt.

'W . . . wolves,' Michael whispered.

'*What?*'

'*Wolves*. Straight ahead.'

He aimed the beam in the same direction, but this time it picked up nothing. He roved it left and right and then behind, but still nothing. But they were there. He knew it. The dogs knew it.

'I don't see . . .'

'They're there!'

'OK, let's not panic . . .'

'I'm not panicking!'

'I didn't say you were, I said—'

'Then shut up! What do we do?'

'We need to make some noise, they're nervous creatures. Make some noise, come on!'

'Get out of here!' Michael shouted. 'Go on . . . get!'

'Louder!' Katya yelled. 'Go on, scram!'

'Get lost! Get the hell away from us!'

'Louder!'

Katya slipped off the sledge and retrieved two of the small saucepans they'd used for heating the beans. She clattered them together, creating a considerable metallic racket.

'Come on, Michael, louder. If they're hungry—'

'I'm shouting as loud as I—'

'Come on! You sound like a little bird! *Louder!*'

'I—'

'LOUDER! OUR LIVES DEPEND ON IT!!'

Something seemed to snap inside him: fear of the wolves, and anger at Katya's grating persistence that he could do better. The sound that now issued from his lungs was like that an angel might make on being cast into the fires of hell. It was so loud and piercing that the dogs tried to bury their heads in the snow.

And he didn't stop.

Michael yelled and cursed and promised to rain all kinds of cruelties on those elusive, invisible, phantom wolves if they dared take a step nearer. He went on and he went on and he went on until his voice was reduced to nothing more than a dry rasp and his eyes looked as if they might pop out of his head. Finally he collapsed on to his knees, clutching at his throat and gasping for breath.

When he glanced up, Katya was standing over him.

'Loud enough?' he whispered.

'I think they probably heard that in Miller's Harbour. You OK? Your face is purple.'

Michael nodded. 'Do you think . . . ?'

Katya took the torch from him and shone it into the fog.

It revealed nothing but solid banks of ghostly grey.

But the dogs were getting back to their feet. They began to snarl at each other, just as they normally did.

The immediate danger had passed.

Chapter Nineteen

Forty minutes later, with the fog just beginning to thin, they found Jordan's sledge. It was on its side, the few supplies he had taken with him spilled out to one side. His rifle was missing. The dogs' traces had been cut and there was a scramble of paw prints leading off to the west. There were several sets of footprints around the sledge, larger than Jordan's.

And on the ground, already frozen black and hard: blood.

'Do you think—' Michael began.

'Shhhh.'

Michael's first inclination was to snap something back. His second was to scan the plain around him as far as the dissipating fog would allow in case she had spotted something. But his third told him to stay quiet. Katya, annoying as she was, had more experience of this kind of thing than he had. She was already crouching down, examining the sledge itself and the tracks surrounding it. Slowly she began to widen the circumference of her inquiry, until she was almost fifty metres out from Jordan's sledge. She dropped to her knees and picked something up. She stayed on her knees and moved in another slowly widening circle until she found something else. Then she hurried back to Michael. She opened her glove and showed him two spent bullet cartridges.

'What're you thinking?'

'I'm thinking whoever was following Jordan has taken a couple of shots at him.'

'How do you know it wasn't the other way round? Or Jordan shooting at the polar bear?'

'No bear tracks, for one. And these cartridges are of a different calibre to Jordan's. Didn't you look at it? Jordan's was a .300 Winchester Magnum. These are from a .30–06 Springfield rifle.'

'OK, fair enough. But it doesn't mean they actually shot him. The blood could easily be from one of the dogs. It might have been the only way to stop the sledge, taking down the lead dog.'

Katya shook her head. 'Look . . .' She led him across to an area of the snow she'd already examined. 'Here's where they stopped their sledge, and here's where they drove away. Notice anything?'

Michael knelt beside the tracks. 'They're slightly deeper?'

'Exactly. There's extra weight on the sledge. They aren't going to take a dead or injured dog with them, they'd just leave it lying. But if they've killed Jordan, or even wounded him, they'd take him with them, because if they buried him in the snow, come summer, the snows melt, the body would be found.'

Michael wasn't convinced. 'Look, if we're right, and they're looking for the Eden, and they're prepared to shoot a teenager, then they're clearly pretty desperate. I don't think they'd have any qualms about killing him and leaving him where he falls. They're bound to have seen the wolves as well, they'd know there wouldn't be much of a body left after those animals were finished with him. So is it not more likely they've taken Jordan with them for a reason?'

'Like what?'

'Like they're lost? And Jordan has a GPS?'

'Then they'd just take the GPS and leave Jordan.' Katya nodded thoughtfully for several seconds, then turned and crossed to the sledge. 'Hey, give me a hand.'

Michael went to the far end and took a firm grip. Together they righted it. Katya gave a muffled clap of her gloved hands as she nodded down. There, crushed into the snow, was the unmistakable outline of Jordan's GPS.

As she crouched to pick it up, Michael hurried up beside her. 'Is it . . . ?'

Katya pulled off one of her gloves with her teeth before jabbing a button. Instantly the screen lit up.

'Do you think he dropped it when he was shot? Or maybe he planted it there?'

'Why would he do that?'

'Because if theirs is broken, and they've shot him, he'll know they're bad guys. He doesn't want to give them any help, he can lead them round in circles until someone comes to help.'

But Katya was shaking her head as she examined the screen. 'Oh, this is not good,' she muttered.

Michael peered down at it. The map was featureless, as were their surroundings, but for two pulsating blips.

'That's us,' said Katya, pointing at one stationary blip. She moved her finger to the other. 'And that has to be the bear.'

'Well, that's good. It's nowhere near us.'

'But look what direction it's going in. And look

where those sledge tracks are heading.' She studied the horizon for the moment, her lips moving almost imperceptibly. 'Those gunshots we heard came from right here about two hours ago. Think about how fast those dogs can move, even with a little extra weight. My guess is right about now, that man-eating bear's going to meet that sledge head on. And with the fog still hanging around, chances are neither of them is going to realize until they're right on top of each other.'

Michael scanned the horizon, squinting through the hazy fog, and nodded slowly.

'Well,' said Katya, 'we better get started after them.'

Michael gave her a half smile. 'You sure you don't want to go for help?'

'Certain,' said Katya.

Chapter Twenty

They were less than a kilometre away when they looked back to see the wolves snapping at each other around the upturned sledge. Neither Michael nor Katya said anything. But they were both thinking the same thing. *What if it's Jordan's blood?*

And if the wolves hadn't had a taste for human blood before, they surely had now.

Katya was on the sledge, facing backwards, her eyes fixed on the wolves, *knowing* that any moment they would turn, sniff the air, and renew their pursuit.

Michael urged the dogs to greater speed. He tried not to think about the fact that they were probably heading towards even greater danger.

There is an old expression about being caught between a rock and a hard place. Michael had always thought of it as applying only to set, inanimate objects.

But these rocks and hard places were anything but motionless – they were constantly shifting, they were cunning and deadly. Hungry wolves chasing down human flesh, a mythical polar bear which had torn a hunter to shreds, and evil men so intent on their mission that they were prepared to shoot and possibly kill a teenage boy.

'I joined SOS for the excitement,' Michael shouted above the yapping of the huskies and the *whoosh* of the sledge runners through the snow, 'but I may be changing my mind!'

Katya nodded grimly. Then her eyes widened and she exhaled a steamy breath. Michael didn't need to look, but couldn't help it.

Yes, indeed. The wolves were coming.

It wasn't a sprint. More like a long-distance race. Thirty minutes further on and flecks of snow began to fall again. Before very long it was coming down in thick sheets. Thankfully there was no accompanying wind to blast it into their faces, but it was still almost unbearably cold. They had all the right gear, but no amount of padding could protect their core temperature indefinitely. It sucked the strength from their muscles. It made them ache and crave the warmth and protection of their tent and cooker. But it was impossible to stop.

They pressed on. The fresh snow sat thick upon the previous night's frozen layer. It was almost sticky in its consistency, which slowed their progress. Michael and Katya had to step off the sledge and lead the dogs from the front. The wolves, driven by hunger and light on their feet, were closing fast.

To make matters worse they were beginning to lose sight of the tracks they were following. Within a very few minutes they were running blind, hoping they were going in the right direction, but ultimately not really caring because the wolves were the real fear now. They caught the briefest glimpses of them through the curtain of snow, each time a little closer. The dog team whimpered as they strained against their traces, seeming to know that they would soon be fighting for their lives. They needed little encouragement to forge ahead, but they just weren't fast enough.

Michael knew they had to do something, something radical. He had a sudden flashback to being stranded on the sinking school bus in the middle of the River Ryburn, with the water cascading past. Their survival had ultimately been down to getting out of the current. And that was what they needed to do now: the sledge was like the river, going in one direction, the wolves like the current, inescapably tied to it.

'Katya! We need to abandon the sledge!'

'What? Are you mad? Out here without . . . !'

'We have no choice! If the dogs keep running the wolves will follow them until they catch up. It might buy us ten, fifteen minutes. We slip away and if we're lucky they won't see us. We can hardly see in front of our faces.'

'But what if you're wrong?'

'Then we get eaten slightly earlier than we might have been.'

'That's not very reassuring!'

Katya looked across at him, but with her face mostly covered by her snow-flecked goggles it was impossible to judge what she was thinking.

'What do we bring?'

'Nothing!'

Katya quickly turned and whacked the lead dog's behind. 'Mush!! Mush!' she yelled and the animal leapt ahead with renewed vigour, dragging the team and sledge with him. Within seconds they had been swallowed up in the swirl.

Katya and Michael turned to their right, ducked down low and began to run as fast as they could, each of them praying silently that the wolves would take the bait and carry on after the sledge.

If anything the snow was deeper, forcing their muscles to work even harder, but they kept going, and going, and going, until they couldn't go any further. Katya's legs were the first to give up, and she collapsed. Michael knelt to help, but found he hadn't the strength to get either of them up again.

They lay on their backs, desperately sucking in air, even though every icy breath felt like they were gargling with jagged glass.

'Do you think . . . ?' Katya whispered.

Michael was too exhausted to reply. Their eyes bore into the curtain of snow.

They lay for fully five minutes, staring.

Then Katya struggled to her feet. 'If we lie here, we die. We have to keep moving.'

Michael pulled himself up beside her. 'Which way?'

'We have to aim for Miller's Harbour. We still have the GPS.'

'What about Jordan?'

'We did our best, Michael. We have to go for help. Or pray it comes for us, because I don't think we're going to make it back if this weather keeps up.'

'I'm not much good at praying,' said Michael.

'Well, maybe you better start practising.'

There was no let-up in the snow. They were freezing. Even through their state-of-the-art gloves and boots their fingers and toes were numb. Michael kept zoning in and out. He was back in his old school, lighting the fire that ultimately burned most of it down. He had lit it because he was cold. Back then, he had *no idea* what being cold really meant.

They forced themselves forward in a steady, draining trudge. Several times they sank into even deeper pockets of snow and wasted crucial time and effort on dragging each other out. Once Michael decided it might be easier just to stay where he was, buried up to his neck in it, and go for a nice sleep. Katya slapped his face and screamed at him and dug him out. Five minutes later he did the same for her.

And then, behind them, the howl of a wolf.

Their ruse had worked, but not for long enough.

They couldn't pick up their pace any further. They were slowing, and the wolves were gaining. They wouldn't have the strength to fight even one wolf off, never mind a pack.

'What do we do?' Michael yelled.

'If we split up, one of us might make it.'

'Is that what you want to do?'

Katya shook her head. 'It would only buy one of us a few extra minutes . . . stick together . . . fight . . .'

She looked back. There were now definitely dark shapes moving towards them. She faltered.

Michael took hold of her hand and pulled her forward, but as he did his feet slipped from under him and he fell, dragging Katya down with him. As they hit the ground they were enveloped by a disgusting stench that immediately made Katya retch.

Michael half laughed and half cried. 'This day isn't getting any better! Wolves about to eat us and now we're covered in . . . crap!'

They were both smeared in it, a big steaming load of it.

The smell was revolting, overpowering – yet seemed too great for the relatively small amount they'd fallen into.

Michael pulled Katya up again. 'Come on!' he screamed. 'Got to keep . . . don't give up . . .'

There was a kind of darkness emerging ahead, like a forest of closely knit trees stretching as far as he could see off to the left and right. But that was impossible. This whole massive island was virtually treeless.

He *had* to be imagining it.

It was surely nothing more than death approaching.

And that seemed more welcome than being torn apart by wolves.

Michael dragged Katya towards its embrace just as the first wolf sank its jagged teeth into her boot. She managed to kick out violently and the wolf dropped back, but only for a moment. As it prepared to renew its attack it was joined by two of its brothers, and they leapt forward together, slavering jaws snapping.

Michael threw himself into the darkness and took Katya with him. They struck something soft, and slipped to the ground.

Feet!

Dozens of them!

Hooves!

The first wolf tried to snap in after them, but was rewarded with a kick which sent it tumbling backwards, yelping. When it came to a stop it instantly leapt back to its feet and snarled, but didn't renew its attack. Instead it loped along the edge of the 'forest', looking for another way in. But the hooves came with legs, and the legs came with bodies, shaggy and stinking but quite, quite wonderful, welcoming bodies topped with long curved and menacing horns.

'*Musk oxen*,' Katya whispered. 'Musk oxen!'

'Musk . . . ?'

'Come on!'

Katya scrambled forward on her hands and knees, carefully dodging between legs and under the close-pressed bodies. There was some grumbling and snorting from the animals, but no stamping or stampeding. When they reached a less tightly pressed area in the middle of the herd they cautiously raised themselves. The animals here were calves, smaller and more nervous, moving back and forth in confusion at being suddenly boxed in.

Michael and Katya gulped for air. A nervous energy born of sudden and unexpected relief flooded through them.

'I don't understand,' Michael panted, 'why aren't they frightened of us or kicking us?'

'Because we smell like them! We've just rolled through musk-ox crap!'

'But the wolves—'

'When the herd is threatened the bulls and cows face outwards and form a stationary ring around the calves. Any wolves that try and break in get kicked to death.'

Michael could scarcely believe it. He knew they weren't *actually* safe, that being marooned in the midst of a herd of musk oxen while wolves prowled around the perimeter was *anything* but safe, but just for this brief moment it felt like they were.

'So what do we do now?'

'We wait. These guys have been protecting themselves against wolves since mammoths were around, they know what they're doing! We stay here among them until the wolves get bored and wander off. Although . . .'

'What?'

'We may have to smear some more stuff on us if we're going to keep fooling the musk oxen into thinking that we're part of the herd.'

Michael looked down. There was lots of it staining the snow around them.

Steaming.

And runny.

'You sure?'

'If you're too squeamish, I'll go first.'

'Who said I was squeamish? It's no problem. Besides, it smells nicer than your perfume.'

Katya made a face.

Michael got down on his knees. He slid one into the mess, and then the next.

'You'd be better lying in it.'

'Give me a chance.'

Michael was busy trying to stop himself from throwing up. He lowered himself down until he was lying on top of it. It squelched underneath him.

'Roll over, get a good covering.'

He rolled. He retched involuntarily.

He slowly got back to his feet.

'OK,' he said, 'your turn.'

Katya smiled triumphantly. 'I was only joking,' she purred. 'We have more than enough on already.'

Chapter Twenty-One

They got used to the stench. They had to. There was no escaping it. The musk oxen were usually docile creatures who looked much bigger than they actually were – beneath their shaggy coats their bodies weren't much bigger than sheep or goats – but they gave an appearance of bulk, their horns were certainly not to be trifled with, and they could kick like . . . well, musk oxen, as more than one wolf discovered. The pack – and Michael counted nine of them, though there might have been more – paced around the stationary, steaming ring for more than an hour, occasionally attempting to break in but getting whacked for their trouble. Eventually they gave up and loped away. But the musk oxen remained resolutely in position.

Peering through the still falling snow Michael said, 'Why aren't they moving? The wolves are gone.'

'Because they're not stupid. Well – probably they *are* stupid, in the sense that they don't know the capital of France or can't tie a knot – but they have thousands of years of instinct to draw on. They'll only break the circle when they know for certain the wolves are gone. What's the visibility, about a hundred metres? They could be waiting, just out of sight.'

So Michael and Katya stayed where they were, even enjoying the surprising warmth that came with having so many bodies pressed together. But they knew it was a temporary respite. They had to come up with a plan for getting back to base, a plan that wouldn't involve them freezing to death.

'We have the GPS, that's the most important thing,' said Katya.

'Why, can we eat it?'

'We've only gone a few hours without food, you idiot.'

'OK. Can we drink it?'

'You're not helping.'

'Sorry. Can we get on top of a couple of these musk oxen and ride them back to base?'

'You could try.'

Michael sighed. Their position was no less hopeless than it had been. They were still marooned on an ice plain, with the snow relentlessly falling. They had no shelter, no supplies, no sledge and no hope of rescue. Plus the wolves were out there, and the polar bear, and the men who had shot and possibly killed Jordan.

Katya's eyes suddenly lit up. She smiled at him.

'We're not finished yet.'

'We're . . . doing a pretty good impression of it. Why . . . what are you . . . ?'

She had knelt down and was now releasing the tabs on her left boot. She pulled it off, then stood up with the boot in her hand.

'Give me five minutes.'

She turned and squeezed into the press of musk oxen surrounding them, pushing forward as far as she could while upright, before dropping down out of sight.

Michael hadn't *a clue* what she was doing.

He stood where he was, occasionally buffeted by the calves.

'Are you . . . Katya . . . ? Are you still . . . ?'

He heard a distant, 'Shhhhh . . .'

A calf nuzzled up against him. He tried not to notice.

'Are you . . . sure musk oxen are . . . like . . . vegetarian?'

'Yes!'

She reappeared five minutes later, carefully cradling

the boot against her chest. She held it out to him. Michael looked at it suspiciously.

'What?'

Katya tilted the boot a little, and a thick, almost brown liquid sloshed over the edge. 'Milk. Musk-ox milk. It's warm, it's full of vitamins.'

Michael looked at her incredulously. 'You want me to drink *that*? You think I'm falling for—'

But Katya cut him off by simply raising the boot to her mouth and gulping greedily. She wiped her glove across her lips.

'It's not a McDonald's milkshake, but it might just save our lives. Four times the fat and protein content of cow's milk.'

She held the boot out to him again.

'You know *far* too much stuff.'

He took hold of it and peered in at the dense liquid. It had a particularly pungent odour.

He took a sip.

It tasted as rotten as it looked.

'Best just to gulp it down,' said Katya.

Michael knew it made sense. He raised the boot to his lips, and began to drink it down as quickly as he could.

'If you come across a toenail,' said Katya, 'I'm missing one.'

The milk exploded out of Michael's face. Katya reeled away, laughing.

'You . . . you are just . . . *evil* . . .'

'You ain't seen nothing yet. Now finish it.'

'Is that an order?'

'Yes.'

Michael poured the rest of the milk on to the ground. It steamed up around him.

'That's what I think of your orders.'

'You are *such* an idiot.'

Gradually the musk oxen began to drift out of their tight formation and wander in a southerly direction. Katya and Michael stayed with them. They were unsure if the threat from the wolves was truly gone and therefore reluctant to depart the comparative safety of the herd. In less than an hour it would be dark and the temperature would plummet even further.

Michael tightened the straps on his gloves and flexed his fingers and toes to pump some blood into them.

'They should be looking for us by now,' he said.

'What if they called or texted the mobile and got Jordan and he was forced to say we were fine?'

'Maybe they've found the Eden, and flown home, and forgotten about us.'

'Forgotten about you, maybe,' said Katya. Then she had a sudden thought. 'No, of course, they're not going to forget about you. You play an important role in SOS. Where would we be without fresh coffee?'

She enjoyed goading him, and was looking for a response, but Michael wasn't even listening. Instead he was standing stiff and alert.

'Michael? What is it?'

'Is it my imagination, or are the muskies picking up speed?'

Katya surveyed the herd. All told, there was about seventy of them, and yes, they did appear restless, and were definitely beginning to increase their pace.

'Maybe they're just nervous,' said Katya.

'Maybe they have reason to be.' Michael's eyes bore into the snow, but there was nothing to see. 'Sooner or later we're going to have to make a break for it. If we stay much longer we're going to become part of the herd. You'll end up having to marry one of them and having little half-human half-musk ox children.'

'I'm starting to think your brain is shutting down, Michael.'

'Still more than enough to—'

But he stopped. They both turned instinctively

in the direction the sound had come from, and it was unmistakable.

A howl.

The wolves were back.

Around them the musk oxen broke into a gallop and, as the panic spread, a charge. Michael and Katya had to throw themselves to one side to avoid being flattened as the herd thundered away.

They lay where they fell, their hearts thumping madly.

'I thought you said they always formed a protective circle,' Michael hissed.

'Apparently, not always,' said Katya.

Their eyes were darting about, trying to pick out the wolves. Another howl came, then another, then barking and snarling. There was no sign of them, but they were getting closer.

'What do we do?'

'Maybe the musk-ox crap will fool them again,' said Katya, but she sounded unconvinced.

'They're not blind.'

Michael got to his feet.

'What're you doing?'

'What does it look like? I'm not going to lie here and wait for them to tear me apart. If they come for me I'm going to face them head on.'

'If they come for you, I'm going to run in the opposite direction.'

'Thanks,' said Michael.

'Don't mention it.'

Without saying anything they moved so that they were standing back to back. The barking and howling grew louder, closer, but with the snow falling thicker than ever and the encroaching darkness it was impossible to make them out.

Michael desperately *wanted* to face them head on, to kick and fight until he was overwhelmed and torn to shreds. But here, at the end, he faltered and the bravado drained out of him. He searched for Katya's glove, found it and gripped it hard. Then he closed his eyes. He didn't want to see those jaws and teeth and evil yellow eyes as they went in for the kill.

But Katya pulled her hand free. Maybe she was braver than he was.

He felt her move from behind him. He twisted to see her bound forward, *towards* the sound of the oncoming wolves.

She was sacrificing herself to give him a chance.

'Katya!' he screamed. 'No!'

He went after her.

She'd barely covered a dozen metres when he threw himself at her, trying to rugby-tackle her, but he missed and she ran on, and now she was clapping her hands and laughing.

She had gone *mad.*

And then he saw what she saw, racing towards them, yapping and barking – their dog team and their sledge, erupting out of the snow as if they were a rescue team sent by SOS itself.

Katya dropped to her knees, still clapping.

At the very last moment she threw herself to one side, because the team had no intention of stopping. It wasn't as pleased to see her as she was to see them, or perhaps they caught a whiff of her and mistook her for a skinny, two-legged musk ox. They raced past her.

Michael was so stunned and surprised that he almost let them escape. Shaking himself just in time, he dived at the sledge. He managed to get a grip on the back of it, but then found himself being dragged along behind it.

He shouted and yelled at the dogs to stop, but they ignored him. Michael tortuously dragged himself up and on to the step at the back and jammed the metal spike brake into the snow. It was too soft and deep to make a huge difference, but it slowed them enough for him to regain control of their traces and haul the lead dog around in a long curve that led them back to Katya.

As he pulled them to a final stop, she was still clapping her hands.

'Well done! Well done!' she shouted. And although she knew better than to try and pet him, she moved closer to the lead dog. 'I knew you'd come back! You're such a good boy!'

Michael cast his eyes over the sledge. The dogs had been roaming around by themselves for hours and hours, but had managed to keep the sledge and its precious cargo of food and shelter upright and intact. They weren't home yet, but their chances of making it there had suddenly improved dramatically.

But from out of the darkness: more howling.

Despair was flooding through Michael.

Oh no, not now . . .

. . . when more huskies appeared, tethered together, but with nothing behind to slow them down.

They raced up to Michael and Katya's team, half of them barking and snarling, ready to pick a fight, the other half happy to play.

'It's Jordan's team!' cried Katya. 'They've been

chasing our lot around! That's why they're so fired up! It's a miracle!'

She was right. It was a miracle.

All thoughts of limping back to Miller's Harbour were suddenly banished from Michael's mind. He was thinking now about how fast a sledge might move with *two* sets of dogs pulling it – how long it would take them to catch up with Jordan and the men who had shot him.

Chapter Twenty-Two

It was, of course, an absolute 'no' from Katya. And, he had to admit, her argument was completely flawless.

'We've escaped being devoured by the skin of our teeth. Our supplies are low, the weather is getting worse instead of better, we've lost track of where Jordan is, we've no weapons to fend off wolves or bears or bad guys, we've no means of communication and the battery warning light on the GPS is flashing. We have to save ourselves while we still can.'

'Agreed,' said Michael.

But she could tell from the way he said it that he didn't really.

Having fed the dogs, they had snapped the tent up to give them a little respite from the snow and the wind, which had picked up again. They had heated beans and franks and Katya had unearthed a single sachet of past-its-sell-by-date hot chocolate.

'Michael, listen to me, we both feel a bit better because we have the dogs back, and the sledge, and we've had something to eat and there's heat in the cooker. But we're down to the last of the gas, the last of the food, and the dogs have had the scrapings from the tins of pemmican. If we don't get back to SOS, we're finished.'

'I know.'

'But?'

'He's still out there.'

'We don't even know that. He may be sitting with his feet up in Miller's Harbour.'

'They shot him.'

'We don't even know *that.*'

'The blood.'

'Could be from a bear, or a wolf. We *don't know*, Michael, and we shouldn't be staking our lives on a guess.'

'You're right.'

'I know.'

They both sat in the darkness, sipping at the remains of the hot chocolate, passing the single cup between them.

Five minutes.

Ten.

Alone with their thoughts.

Then Katya said, 'We need to go after Jordan.'

'We do.'

'You're thinking two dog teams, twice as fast?'

'I am.'

'I don't know if the leaders will work together. You can't have two bosses.'

'Works for us.'

'You think?'

'Well, we can try.'

'Yes, we can. As long as you agree I'm always right.'

'Don't start.'

They were each bitten twice. At first they kept the two teams separate, running left and right of the sledge, but it proved impossible to control them. Then they put Jordan's team ahead of their own, with the two leaders at the front, but it was simply too great a distance between the leaders and the sledge and besides, the leaders were too busy fighting with each other to pay any attention to commands.

'This isn't going to work,' Katya said. 'Maybe we'd be better—'

'It'll work,' Michael said firmly.

This time he reorganized the teams into four columns, but leaving the two leaders out entirely.

'What're you—'

'You were right. Two bosses doesn't work.'

He set Jordan's leader free. Then he released his rival. In a split second they were rolling in the snow, tearing at each other. Their howls set off the other dogs as well.

Blood spattered on to the ground. Katya turned her face away.

But within a minute Jordan's leader was on top, with his teeth to the other dog's throat. It squirmed helplessly.

Michael stepped in and pulled the winner off, leaving their own leader panting and whining in the snow, defeated. He dragged them both forward, and tethered the beaten dog to the front of the team, and then Jordan's victorious husky in front of him again. They now had a leader, a second-in-command, and a powerhouse of four short teams behind.

Katya snapped down and stowed the tent and grabbed the driver's position at the back. Michael slipped into position on the sledge.

'Think this will work?' Katya asked.

'Absolutely no idea,' said Michael.

'Well,' said Katya, 'only one way to find out.'

The dogs were fired up and ready. She could feel the whole sledge trembling beneath her. She released the brake and was about to yell 'Mush, mush!', but didn't need to. The dogs simply *took off.*

Michael grinned back at her.

It was as if they'd swapped a nice family car for a Ferrari.

They couldn't possibly continue at such a high speed; the dogs would have become exhausted too quickly. Katya gradually slowed them down until they were moving at a good, steady pace, which was still much quicker than what they would have managed with just their own team.

Michael studied the fast-fading GPS and shouted directions.

'The bear doesn't seem to be moving!'

'Is that good or bad?'

'I don't know!'

'How far?'

'Sixteen K!'

'At this speed, that's about an hour!'

'I'll let you know when we're getting close!'

Thirty minutes later Michael felt the sledge slow

beneath him, and looked up from the GPS, surprised.

'What? What is it? We're not—'

'Look.'

The snow was still swirling around them, so it was difficult at first to pick out what Katya was pointing at: but then he saw it, a little lick of colour flickering in and out of the black and white Arctic night.

'Fire?'

'Think so.'

'No one's going to have a camp fire, night like this. Something's burning.'

'We need to get a closer look, but if we take the dogs they'll hear us. This far away, downwind, we should be OK leaving them here. Agreed?'

'Agreed.'

They drove the anchor spike through the layers of fresh snow until they hit the ground below, then between them screwed and twisted it in until it felt secure. The dogs yapped and howled as they set off, but before they'd walked thirty metres their cries were swallowed up by the wind.

Katya asked where the bear was in relation to the fire. Michael said it was impossible to tell. The tracking device was blinking, as if the animal was standing still, but that might only mean that it was stationary within a certain area. And as they'd no fix on the fire beyond what they could see, they were almost literally in the dark.

'But I don't have a good feeling about this,' said Michael.

'That may be the musk-ox milk,' said Katya.

'This isn't funny. I got into this because I set fire to my school, and then I jumped into a frozen river. Fire and ice. The story of my life.'

'Well, let's just hope the story isn't over. Or it has a happy ending.'

'You're the expert – what are we supposed to do if a bear attacks?'

'Lie down, stay still.'

'And if he starts gnawing at my leg?'

'Hop it.'

'That isn't funny either.'

'I know.'

She was smiling through horribly chapped lips.

'We're not a bad team,' said Michael.

'Nope,' said Katya.

They trudged on.

Michael said, 'By "nope" did you mean we're not a bad team, or were you disagreeing with me, or did you mean something else?'

'I meant as long as you understand that I'm in charge, then nope, we're not a bad team.'

'If the bear starts gnawing your leg, I'm leaving you.'

'He'll be too busy gnawing at yours.'

The light ahead, which they'd both been watching, suddenly winked out.

They both stopped.

'What you think?' Michael asked. 'The wind?'

'Maybe. It's getting stronger.'

'Or they could be on the move.'

'Go back for the dogs, or press on?'

Michael looked back, and then forward. As far as he could tell they were about equidistant between the two.

'Let's check it out, another five minutes should get us there. If they're gone we can still catch them up. We've twice the dog power they have.'

They started again, fear growing on them with each step. They began to catch the odd, stray whiff of burning, and with it some kind of odd chemical smell. Then, finally, they saw several dark objects ahead of them, though it was impossible to make out what they were. Michael and Katya dropped to their bellies in the snow and focused in, checking for movement.

'Anything?'

Michael shook his head.

'OK. Let's be careful.'

They raised themselves and crept forward. About twenty metres further on they came across sledge tracks. Katya knelt and ran her fingers across them. She nodded at Michael before rising and they continued on.

They entered what had clearly been a camp – to the left the tattered remains of a tent blew like an abandoned flag, its edges black and burned but already cold to the touch. Inside there were two torn sleeping bags and an upturned stove. The chemical smell was extremely powerful.

'Some kind of fuel?' Michael speculated. 'It's burning my throat.'

'Me too.'

Then they found the body.

He was lying face down. The pool of blood coming from beneath his head had frozen in a jagged semi-circle.

When they turned him Katya let out a little cry. Most of his throat had been torn out.

The only good thing about it was that it wasn't Jordan.

'Recognize him?' Katya asked.

'He's one of them, one of the fake television crew.'

Katya pointed at the ground around his body. 'Look . . . there . . . and there . . . those are polar bear prints . . . they're *huge*.'

Michael crouched beside them. He traced their outline with the fingers of his gloved hand.

'Looks like Jordan's grandfather may have been telling the truth.' He spotted something on the ground and went to pick it up. 'And someone's short of a boot. Out here, unprotected, he'll soon . . .'

He picked it up. And just as quickly dropped it. 'Jesus!'

Katya came up beside him and looked down. 'What . . . ?'

'There's a foot still in it.'

She wasn't perturbed at all. She looked back at the body. It still had both feet. She studied the ground again and soon picked up a trail of blood and scuffed snow and bear prints leading beyond the remains of the tent and on out into the darkness.

Michael watched as she stood perfectly still, surveying the scene, little plumes of steam issuing from her nose. She really was quite cool and composed. It wasn't necessarily a bad way to be in this kind of situation. In fact, he wished he was more like her. His whole body was shaking, and it wasn't just from the cold.

'What puzzles me – why no gunshots?' Michael asked. 'Why didn't they shoot the bear?'

'Panic? Surprise?'

'I only saw those guys for a couple of minutes back at the hotel, but they didn't look the panicking kind. Big, strong guys, smart enough to put Mr Crown in a coma.'

'I'm thinking you may be right,' said Katya.

'What else are you thinking?'

'I'm thinking they set up camp and cooked some food. Bear smelt it and came charging in. It knocked over the stove and set the tent on fire. They scramble out of the tent, but the bear catches one of them, tears his throat out. He catches one of the others and bites his foot off. Decides he's a bit tastier and drags him away to eat in peace and quiet somewhere out there. That leaves one bad guy, and Jordan. The sledge is gone, so we can only presume they escaped . . . but in which direction, and are they together?'

Katya and Michael began to examine the ground surrounding the camp. It was Michael who found the tracks, heading north. Katya bent to examine them. She pushed her goggles up and pulled off a glove. She ran her fingers over the grooves in the snow, then switched to tracing the foot and paw prints. She was shaking her head, but probably wasn't even aware of it.

'What's wrong?' Michael asked.

'We know there were three bad guys, and that two of them are almost certainly dead. But look, two sets of footprints. That's one bad guy, and the others have to be Jordan's.'

'OK, so if he was shot, then he's recovered enough to walk.'

'But look at the tracks. They're twice as deep as they were even when Jordan was being carried. They're in a panic to get away, they have a full dog team, yet neither of them is on the sledge.'

Michael nodded beside her. 'Because there's no room. They're carrying something big and heavy.'

'Something that accounts for the chemical smell.'

Michael pushed his goggles up.

'You thinking what I'm thinking?'

Katya nodded.

And then they said it together.

'They've found the Eden!'

Chapter Twenty-Three

There was, of course, no *definitive* evidence that they'd found the Eden. There was suspicion, and they guessed that that overpowering chemical smell was the highly toxic hydrazine propellant leaking from the downed satellite, but they wouldn't really know until they saw it with their own eyes – which was exactly what they intended to do.

They hurried back to the sledge, the wind at their backs helping to speed them along. That, and pure excitement.

'The Eden . . . we'll be heroes,' Michael said.

'We have to remain focused . . .'

'The best technology money can buy, helicopters, satellite tracking, and *we* find it . . .'

'We *haven't*, not yet, anyway. If they've found it then they must have better equipment than SOS, better than NASA. They must be a pretty powerful outfit.'

'They may be – but they still can't control the weather, that's why they had to send a dog team and sled to get hold of it.'

'They have a head start on us. They have guns,' Katya snapped.

'We have speed, if we're careful we might have surprise. We can *do* this . . .'

'It might not even be the Eden. It could be anything.'

'Like?'

'Like I don't know . . . a sea elephant.'

'Yeah, right,' Michael retorted. 'One just dropped down from the sky. It's the Eden, I know it is. I don't care what you say, I'm not going back to base now. This is ours, we have to go for it.'

'I know.' She was as excited as he was.

'You *know*? Seriously? I thought you'd be all for getting SOS on the case. Not that we're not SOS.'

'That would be the best course of action. But we don't have time.'

'Meaning?'

'Meaning I don't exactly know who the bad guys are, or were – but they must have had a plan. I can't believe they just accidentally stumbled across the Eden. They had a good idea of where to look, but something went wrong, they got lost. But they must have had an exit strategy, some plan for getting the Eden out of here once they found it. They weren't just going to turn up at Miller's Harbour airport with it in their hand baggage, were they? I'm thinking they need to call in help, I'm thinking that if their own communications are down, they still have the mobile phone Jordan took off me. With the weather they haven't been able to get a signal, but it could lift any time; in a few minutes or a few hours, they can summon a chopper and get out of here with the Eden before anyone realizes. *That's* why we have to go and stop them.'

'OK,' said Michael, 'if you insist.'

They had speed, they had adrenaline, they had expectation and they had fear. They had dreams and they had nightmares. What they didn't have was a plan, because there was nothing they could plan *for*. They knew what they were doing was foolish and dangerous, but also that it was essential. It was so much bigger than rescuing Jordan or proving what they could do for SOS. It was about the Eden. About contributing to something that was bigger than themselves, bigger than SOS, bigger than states, countries and continents. It was about the entire planet.

Retracing their steps with the dogs this time, they reached the camp with the burned-out tent and the boot with the foot. They picked up the sledge tracks on the far side. With the snow and wind the tent would not have burned for long, which meant that their quarry could not be too far ahead.

Though the snow continued to fall, it was beginning to lighten. Above them the first star was visible. Before very long the moon poked through a break in the clouds, lighting the whole plain in a sudden jet of light, like the search light in a prison camp. It made them even more nervous, but it didn't slow them down.

Then they spotted something incongruous, perhaps 1500 metres away.

'What is it?' Michael shouted.

Katya just shook her head. It was impossible to tell.

She guided the dogs off the sledge tracks and swung them wide of the object, so that they could circle round and get a better look without getting too close.

'Sledge?'

'Looks like it,' said Michael.

Their own dogs, catching the scent of the other team, began to bark and growl. A single figure was sitting on the seat, but it wasn't moving.

'Think it's Jordan?'

'I can't see,' said Katya.

'Maybe the other guy's gone. With the weather breaking maybe he's been picked up, taken the Eden with him.'

'If it's Jordan, why isn't he moving, why's he just sitting there?'

'Maybe he's . . . ?'

'Don't. I didn't hear a shot.'

'Maybe he didn't shoot him. Stabbed him or strangled him. Maybe he was shot before and he's finally—'

'We can talk if and maybes all night, Michael. We have to go in.'

'Try shouting to him first.'

'And what if the other guy hears it? He might come storming back and shoot us.'

'OK. Then *let's go*.'

Katya steered the double team away from their circular path and aimed for the immobile sledge.

The moon obligingly re-emerged as they drew closer, and they could now see that it definitely was Jordan on the sledge – but he still wasn't moving. And he was perched on something large which glistened with a metallic sheen when the moonlight caught it.

The Eden.

Michael felt another surge of adrenaline. They were so close to laying claim to it.

About twenty metres short they spiked the sledge and cautiously moved forward, Katya a little to the left of Jordan's sledge, Michael to the right.

'Jordan?' Katya called. 'Are you OK?'

His goggles were on and his hood up.

No response.

'*Jordan . . .*' Michael hissed. 'Is it safe?'

Still nothing.

When they were just ten metres short of him, Jordan's hand finally moved.

They both stopped.

Jordan pushed his goggles up off his face.

'Jordan?' said Katya.

'You OK?'

It felt like it took an eternity for him to respond.

'Sorry,' he said.

'Sorry?' said Michael.

Jordan's eyes flitted to his left. As they did the snow there began to move, and a shape erupted from it – a man in a white snowsuit, with a rifle aimed at them, and a thin cruel smile on his face.

They had walked into a trap.

Michael and Katya raised their arms.

Jordan said, 'I'm sorry, he made me . . .'

And then toppled forward.

As he hit the ground Katya leapt towards him.

'Stay where you are!'

But she ignored him.

The man fired. The bullet bit into the snow at her feet. But she didn't stop.

Katya skidded to a halt beside Jordan and dropped to her knees. As she knelt over him and began to turn him over the man with the gun strode forward and cracked her once with the butt of his rifle on the side of her head. She keeled over, knocked out cold.

Michael took a step forward, but the man spun towards him, gun raised again and trained on his chest.

'I dare you,' said the man.

Michael stopped where he was. Both sets of dogs, set off by the shot, were barking madly. Katya lay unmoving on her back beside Jordan. The young Inuit was labouring for breath. There was a trickle of frozen blood in the corner of his mouth.

'I need to . . . help them . . .' Michael said.

'You don't need to do anything besides bring your sledge over.'

'My sledge . . . why?'

'I don't need you to ask questions either. Just bring over the damn sledge.'

He indicated with his rifle where he wanted it positioned, but in moving his arm Michael saw that there was a long tear in his snowsuit, and a bloody gash was just visible.

Michael turned and began to trudge towards his sledge. Behind him the man shouted, 'You try anything, I shoot you in the head.'

What could he even think about trying? He had no weapon, nowhere to run or hide. He glanced back. The man was examining a mobile phone. Beside him Jordan was coughing and had managed to get himself on to his side. There was something about the sledge he'd fallen off: it looked lopsided. That was it, then: the weight of the Eden had caused one of the runners to buckle.

Michael pulled the spike out, stepped up behind his sledge, and guided the dogs the few dozen metres across to where Jordan and Katya lay. As soon as the two dog teams met there was a renewed frenzy of barking. The man in the torn snowsuit strode between them, battering left and right with the butt of his gun in a fruitless attempt to quieten them down. Their howls of pain only contributed to the cacophony.

'Quiet! Quiet, you mangy sons of . . . !' The man broke off and checked his mobile phone again. He was either waiting for a message or checking the time. He smiled. 'Right,' he snapped out, 'you need to give me a hand shifting this.' He nodded at the Eden. 'Know what it is?'

Michael shook his head.

The man laughed. 'Then you never will.'

Michael had seen photos of the Eden, all shiny and new, a magnificent collection of antennas, receivers and transmitters, of beacons, transponders, dishes and sensors. But now it was blackened, battered and dripping a black noxious substance that had clearly failed to freeze. It looked more like something that might be rejected by a scrap yard. He didn't know if the damage had been caused by it being shot down, or by its re-entry into Earth's atmosphere, but he did know that its value no longer rested in what it was capable of recording about the state of the planet, but in its very existence. And that the longer it remained out in the snow, the longer it would continue to leak poison into the environment. None of this concerned this man, whoever he was, whoever he was working for, he only wanted the Eden so that it could be completely destroyed and the cause that it was launched for further delayed or derailed.

'Move it!'

They each took a grip of the fallen satellite. But the man was hampered because he was trying to hold on to his rifle. He shifted it to his wounded arm, but wasn't happy with that either. Finally he set it on the ground, and took hold of the Eden with both hands. He nodded across at Michael.

'Don't even think about trying anything stupid. I could break you like a twig. Now, on the count of three. One, two, three . . .'

They both heaved, and the Eden came up surprisingly easily. They shuffled the few metres across to Michael and Katya's sledge. But the man, in his anxiety to get moving, hadn't thought it through properly. There was no room on the sledge to set it down.

'Put it down, put it down!'

They lowered the Eden on to the snow. The man hurriedly undid the straps securing the supplies and equipment on the second sledge before kicking everything off.

'Right, now, lift!'

This time they successfully manoeuvred it into place, and the man clicked the straps to secure it. He stepped back and looked at his mobile phone. Then he lifted it to his ear.

'Rendezvous in twenty minutes at our agreed coordinates. How many passengers?' His eyes flitted up to Michael. 'Just me.'

He closed the phone and slipped it into his coat pocket. He crouched to retrieve the rifle.

Michael said, 'You can't leave us out here without a sledge.'

'I don't intend to.'

The man checked that his rifle was fully loaded. Then he raised it and pointed it at Michael.

So that was it. He was going to be murdered.

'You're just going to . . . kill me?'

'No. I'm going to kill all of you.'

'But—'

'It'll be quick.'

'But . . . *why*?'

'Why will it be quick? It's the nature of bullets.'

The man was laughing. Playing with him. And he had no reason not to. He had what he'd come for. He was about to kill the only witnesses and then be whisked away back to civilization. He held all the cards. He didn't know Michael. As far as he was aware he was just some kid who'd stumbled into a conspiracy.

Michael wanted to say something. His last words. Something profound about dying in a good cause: trying to protect the planet. He wanted to shout out that he was proud to be part of SOS, and that he had had a grand adventure with Katya and Jordan, and he had done his best. And that whoever this man with the gun was, whoever was coming to take him and the Eden away, he hoped they knew that they could never win.

He *wanted* to shout all of this, and much more besides, but for the life of him all he was really thinking was:

Don't shoot me.

Please don't shoot me.

The man had slipped his glove off to give him better purchase on the trigger.

All Michael could think about *now* was the fact that his killer had fat fingers.

Fat fingers.

His whole life about to end, and all he could summon for his last ever thought was:

Fat fingers.

He focused on them, and then the rifle, wondering if he would see the bullet, if he would feel it explode into his skull.

And then he was back to fat fingers.

Murdered by the fat-fingered man.

He was a tall man, well muscled, with erect, military bearing. You could train and train and train, but if God gave you fat fingers, you were stuck with them.

The dogs suddenly erupted in another frenzy of barking, causing the fat-fingered man a moment's hesitation as he glanced at them.

But just as quickly he was back focused on Michael.

He squeezed the trigger.

But at that very point where death would be unleashed, there came a huge roar from the gunman's left.

The fat-fingered man began to swing towards it – but he was too late.

A polar bear, *the* polar bear, bigger and stronger and more savage than any bear had ever been, a polar bear with massive jaws already dyed red from its feeding frenzy, its yellow teeth dripping with blood, swept a mighty paw across the fat-fingered man's head, knocking him sideways and the gun out of his hands.

The man landed flat on his back with a *whump*, the breath knocked from him and his senses hopelessly scrambled. The bear rose to its full height, threw his head back and roared. The man pulled himself up to his knees and looked groggily around him. He spotted his rifle and began to crawl towards it. Michael watched helplessly. The bear watched as well – almost as if he couldn't believe the man still had the strength to move. Centimetre by centimetre he crawled towards the weapon, seemingly unaware that the bear was now looming over him. And then, just as he reached out to grab hold of it, the bear struck again, one paw swiping down and knocking the man on to his back, and then with mesmerizing speed his teeth tore savagely into his throat. The man's legs began a mad kind of dance and his arms flailed helplessly. The fat-fingered man's screams ended abruptly.

The dogs, terrified, took off, dragging the sledge and the Eden with them.

Michael stood frozen to the spot.

As soon as the fat-fingered man's body stopped convulsing, the bear lost interest. Michael knew that the creature had feasted already that night. It couldn't be hunger that was driving him now, but a desire to kill.

It turned, veins and flesh and bone hanging from its mouth.

It saw Michael.

It threw its head back and howled.

It was truly a monster.

The rifle, knocked from the fat-fingered man's hands as he fell, was on the other side of the bear.

There was nothing Michael could do.

There had been something clinical about the threat of being shot. His death would have been so quick.

But this would be *horrible*.

He could run, but he would be caught and torn to shreds.

The bear roared again.

It advanced on all fours.

All the power went out of Michael's legs. He dropped to his knees. He bowed his head and closed his eyes.

The bear loomed over him.

Its jaws moved towards his face.

Its ghastly rotten-meat breath enveloped him.

It raised itself up and roared.

And then, from behind, something so unexpected:

Jordan, pushing himself up on one elbow, blood still drooling from his mouth, began to sing.

Sing, or chant.

Something haunting, something as ancient and mythical as the creature that towered above Michael. Something Michael could not understand. Something that made the creature hesitate.

It felt like an eternity – the bear's teeth so close, the drip, drip, drip of blood on to the snow, the bitter cold, the brightness of the moon, the sheer infinite beauty of the stars in a now cloudless sky. Jordan's voice was so pure, so lyrical. It wasn't even loud, but it seemed to travel for ever, across the ice plain, up to those stars.

The bear looked to Jordan.

It seemed to shake its head, as if waking from a dream, and then, gloriously, it began to pad slowly away.

Jordan continued to sing until his breath grew laboured, and he began to stumble over the words, and then he slumped down, and everything was silent.

Michael stared after the bear, terrified that once the singing had stopped the spell would be broken, and it would return, more fearsome than ever.

But it kept going, and did not look back.

Michael finally, finally let out his breath.

He was in the middle of a desolate snow plain, there was a savagely mutilated body beside him, his two friends were unconscious, and his sledge and the dogs were gone.

But he felt incredible.

Lucky and blessed.

He wasn't finished yet.

Not by a long shot.

Chapter Twenty-Four

'Dr Kincaid! Dr Kincaid!'

'Dr Kincaid! Will you answer the question!'

'Dr Kincaid!'

The press conference was becoming chaotic, and Dr Kincaid, in the blinding glare of television lights, with close to sixty reporters packed into the restaurant in the Miller Hotel, was doing his best to remain calm and collected. He knew the truth, and he knew the journalists knew the truth, but he was doing his best to avoid giving a straight answer, and they were doing their best to catch him out.

The truth was that their mission to the Arctic in pursuit of the Eden satellite had been a disaster. Not only had they produced no evidence that it had survived the explosion that followed its launch, they had failed to find the 'so-called' wreckage, they had failed to produce evidence that it had been shot down in the first place, and now rumours were circulating that two members of SOS and a native guide had perished after being caught in a blizzard.

Dr Kincaid pointed out into the throng. 'I'm sorry, could you repeat the question?'

'Dr Kincaid, have you any evidence at all to back up any of your claims, or has this all been one big publicity stunt for SOS?'

Dr Kincaid put on his best smile and said, 'Well, if it's a publicity stunt, it's not working very well, is it?'

'But do you have any evidence?'

'The evidence is out there, we remain convinced of that, but we have been hampered in our attempts to find it. This has to do with the appalling weather, which we have all struggled to deal with, and also several acts of sabotage to both our helicopters and our fleet of snowmobiles, which has severely restricted our efforts to locate the Eden.'

'Sabotage? Is it not the case that you just are not equipped for these conditions, and that you've been making wild claims without a single shred of evidence?'

Dr Kincaid was doing his best not to get exasperated. 'We aren't in the business of making wild claims. And our equipment is state of the art. Next question?'

'Is it not also true that you allowed two teenagers, two schoolchildren, to travel with you to Miller's Harbour, that they were left unsupervised, and that they are now missing in what is some of the worst weather this part of the world has ever seen?'

'No.'

'They're not missing? We were told—'

'The teenagers are junior members of SOS. They were . . . they *are* on an educational mission which is part of their training. They are supervised by a local guide, they are fully trained in survival techniques and we have been tracking them throughout. They are not in the slightest bit of danger.'

A different reporter shouted, 'Is it not true that the leader of your so-called Artists slipped on the ice and has spent the last three days in a coma?'

'Thank you for your concern. Our team leader, Mr Crown, was assaulted by person or persons unknown shortly after arriving in Miller's Harbour. He remains in a critical con—'

'Actually, I'm feeling just fine.'

Every head, including Dr Kincaid's, turned towards the doors at the back of the restaurant. Mr Crown was standing there, resplendent in his SOS uniform, looking as grim as ever, with just a string of fresh-looking stitches above his left eye to indicate that he had suffered any kind of an injury.

Bailey, Bonsoir and Dr Faustus stood beside him.

'As you can see,' said Dr Kincaid, trying hard to mask his relief, 'Mr Crown is very far from being in a coma.'

Crown strode through the throng. Reporters jumped out of his way. The other Artists followed him to the front of the restaurant and joined Dr Kincaid on the low, makeshift stage. Stepping on to it gave Crown even greater height. His sheer physical presence dominated the room. And when his voice boomed out across it, everyone listened, and everyone obeyed.

'Dr Kincaid has answered all of your questions with remarkable patience. We're here to do a job. We've been hampered by weather, but soon as it breaks, we'll be out there, and we will find the Eden, that I promise. That's all we have to say. This press conference is now over.'

'But who attacked you?' one of the reporters shouted.

Crown fixed him with a withering look. 'I said it was over,' he snapped.

With that he turned to Dr Kincaid, and they exchanged nods. Dr Kincaid led the Artists off the stage and out of the doors at the back of the restaurant, waving and smiling for the cameramen as he went. But as soon as they hit the stairs leading up to their temporary HQ in the conference room on the first floor the smile slipped away and his features became grim and set.

'Welcome back,' he said to Mr Crown. 'How's the head?'

'It's fine.'

'I tried to insist on forty-eight hours' further bed rest,' said Dr Faustus, 'but he ignored me. As usual.'

'I'm fine,' Mr Crown repeated.

'Apart from the fact that up until about ten minutes ago you couldn't remember why we were here in the Arctic, let alone who attacked you!'

'Relax, Doc, would you?' said Crown.

Dr Faustus looked at Dr Kincaid and shrugged helplessly.

'I've updated him on the situation,' said Bonsoir.

'So you'll know it's not good,' said Dr Kincaid as they entered the busy HQ. 'Those kids, I should never . . .' He trailed off. 'Is there no hope of finding them?'

'We were tracking Katya's mobile intermittently until about nine hours ago,' said Bonsoir. 'It put them about eighty kilometres from here, but there's been nothing since. Repeatedly tried to speak to her over the past forty-eight hours, but nothing, no texts.'

'What do you think – what's the best case scenario?'

'They're holed up somewhere, waiting for the storm to pass. Can't get a signal, or the battery died.'

'Worst case?'

'Out there, you make a mistake, you pay with your life.'

Dr Kincaid shook his head. 'This is terrible. Terrible for them, terrible for us, terrible for the entire SOS. It's a public relations disaster!' He strode on across the room, already whipping out his phone to make another call.

Mr Crown shook his head after him.

At his elbow Bailey said, 'If only this damn weather would lift, I know I could find them!'

He slapped his fist angrily into his hand before turning and crossing to the window. He stared out across the few buildings that stood between the hotel and the huge expanse of snow beyond. A moment later he felt a heavy hand on his shoulder.

'Hey,' said Mr Crown, 'from what Bonsoir tells me, you've already flown half a dozen suicide missions out there looking for them. You've done everything you can.'

'It's not enough.'

'We've had casualties before, and we'll have them again. It goes with the territory.'

He patted him again, then turned away. He crossed to one computer to check on the weather forecast, then to another to check through a series of satellite photographs they'd been sent by a friendly government's spy satellite which had flown over the island when there'd been a brief break in the clouds; but there was no trace of Michael, Katya or the Eden. The only photograph that showed anything other than plain white snow was one of a pack of wolves surrounding a herd of musk oxen.

When Mr Crown glanced back up, Bailey was still standing at the window. But he was no longer looking upset, or staring vaguely out into nothingness; his face was almost pressed against the glass. He turned suddenly.

'Anyone got binoculars?'

One of the computer analysts opened a drawer, produced a pair and hurried them across to him.

As Bailey focused in, Mr Crown came up beside him. 'What is it?'

'I'm not . . . sure . . . look, what do you make of it?'

Bailey handed the binoculars to his colleague. Mr

Crown raised them to his eyes and scanned what appeared to be a blank vista.

'Can't see any—'

There, on the far left, there was movement.

Something long, thin. As if someone had drawn a snake on a whiteboard. A snake with multiple heads.

'Not sure what it is . . .'

'Let me see.' It was Bonsoir, coming up beside them. 'Twenty euros says I identify first. I got the best eyesight by far.'

Mr Crown offered him the glasses. 'Twenty euros says you don't. You have another ten seconds.'

As Bonsoir worked the focus, Dr Faustus joined them.

'You guys will bet on anything,' he said. 'I'll hand over forty euros if I don't get it in the next ten.'

Bonsoir lowered the glasses. 'I'm always willing to earn easy money.'

As Dr Faustus raised the glasses, Dr Kincaid came wandering over.

'Haven't you guys anything better to be doing?'

The only response he got came from Dr Faustus. 'It's a sledge, guys. Never seen one with that many dogs. Gee, must be nearly twenty . . .'

Dr Kincaid said, 'Let me see.'

'If it's agreed I get the money.'

But Dr Kincaid wasn't playing. He snapped his fingers impatiently.

Dr Faustus sighed and handed them over. 'You're the boss,' he said, before grinning at his other colleagues. 'You all owe me, big time.'

'No way,' Bailey began. 'Anyone could have guessed—'

Dr Kincaid cut him off with an urgent, '*Shhhhhh* . . .'

They obediently fell silent.

Dr Kincaid said nothing for fully thirty seconds.

And then:

'Well, I'll be . . .'

'What is it?' Mr Crown asked.

Dr Kincaid lowered the glasses and rubbed at his eyes, as if he couldn't quite believe what he was seeing. Then he fixed them back in place and studied the scene for another ten seconds before exploding:

'It's them, it's only bloody them!'

Dr Kincaid thrust the binoculars into Mr Crown's hands, spun on his heels and headed for the stairs.

A moment later, Dr Faustus went after him.

Then Bailey.

And Bonsoir.

Only Mr Crown was left at the window. He raised the binoculars and focused in.

Then he started laughing.

It was so deep and booming, so unexpected and so out of character, that everyone else in HQ stopped their work to look at him.

When he finally turned and hurried towards the stairs, they knew that something important was happening. They got up from their desks and followed. At first they moved quite calmly, but then as their excitement grew it turned into something of a stampede. The journalists downstairs, busy filing their reports or discussing how big a mess SOS had made of the situation, became aware first of the tremendous thundering coming from the stairs, and then saw everyone rushing out of the hotel, and they followed. The camera crews grabbed their cameras and charged out on to the slushy Main Street.

Dr Kincaid had stopped a hundred metres up. Dr Faustus came to a skidding halt beside him and was quickly joined by the other Artists. SOS staff crowded in behind, jostled by reporters and finally camera crews as the sledge, pulled by an almost inconceivably large team of dogs, hove into view and continued its steady pace towards them.

And there was Michael, his hood down, his goggles up, a smile plastered across his face, standing at the back, mushing the dogs along. In front of him sat Katya, her goggles also pushed up, holding Jordan secure in her arms. The Inuit boy's eyes were closed. His face was dreadfully pale and with the bulk of his coat it was impossible to tell if he was even breathing.

As he brought the sledge to a halt Michael jumped off the back step.

'Dr Faustus!' he shouted. 'It's Jordan . . . !'

The doctor hurried forward.

'He's been shot,' said Katya, 'he's unconscious . . . please do something . . .'

'It's OK, we've got him now . . .'

As Dr Faustus signalled for SOS volunteers to help him lift Jordan into the hotel, Dan Nappaaluk pushed through the crowd.

'Jordan!' he cried, and knelt beside Dr Faustus. 'Jordan.' He took hold of his son's hand. 'What have you done to him?'

'He saved our lives!' said Michael.

'We found the bear . . . !' said Katya. She stopped suddenly, as if surprised at herself for shouting out. But then she continued. She couldn't help it. It was as if someone had shaken a bottle of Coke and then whipped off the lid. 'The bear! The giant bear! It killed them! Three of them! The bad guys! The ones who found the—'

Dr Kincaid cut her off. 'Killed? Killed who? Katya . . . Michael . . . what on earth have you been up to . . . ?'

Michael, still trying to catch his breath, could hardly speak. 'It's . . . a long . . . story . . .'

As Jordan was lifted off her, Katya pulled herself up off the sledge. She stood up – but then staggered forward. Dr Faustus caught her and steadied her. He saw now that the top of her cheek was bruised and swollen.

'Are you OK?'

'Yes . . . fine . . . a little . . .'

Her eyes looked unfocused. Dr Faustus shook his head. 'Right, we need to get a proper look at you too.' He turned to address the crowd. 'Can we make room, get these kids indoors?'

'No . . . *wait* . . .' Katya took a deep breath, then pulled herself up erect. 'I'm OK, I'm OK. We . . . have to do something first . . .'

'Young lady, you are in no state to—'

'Just *wait*!'

Dr Faustus held his hands up. 'OK.'

'I'm sorry,' said Katya. 'We just need to . . .' She

nodded at Michael. 'Do you want to do this now . . . ?'

'Maybe we should keep it for later? Build up the suspense.'

'Don't know if I can stand up for much longer.'

'Good point.'

Dr Kincaid stepped between them. 'I don't know what you two are on about, but if you've anything to tell us, like what the hell you think you were playing at going out there without . . .' He stopped himself. 'You two have a lot of explaining to do, but best do it out of the glare of these cameras. Let's get inside and—'

'Not yet,' said Katya.

'*What?*'

Dr Kincaid liked to portray himself as the easy-going and approachable head of SOS, but he wasn't used to having his instructions ignored, and he didn't like it one little bit.

'We'll go in a minute,' said Michael.

'You'll go when I damn well—'

'We thought you'd like your present first,' said Katya.

'*What?* Present?' Dr Kincaid shook his head and turned to Dr Faustus. 'Doctor, have you some kind of sedative? They're clearly not making sense . . .'

But Dr Faustus wasn't paying any attention to him either. He was watching Katya and Michael. They were taking hold of a sleeping bag they had opened up and secured across the bottom half of their sledge.

'We thought . . .' Katya began.

'That you might like to see this,' Michael finished.

He nodded. Katya nodded. They whipped the sleeping bag away.

Dr Kincaid just stared.

They *all* just stared.

'It's the Eden,' Michael said, needlessly.

Epilogue

As part of his debriefing at the Miller Hotel, Dr Faustus had suggested to Michael that he draw up a mental list of exactly how he was feeling at that moment in time, because it would be good to have something positive to draw on in the future when he was in another sticky situation.

Michael had just blinked at him. He hadn't even *considered* the possibility that there might be a next time.

Why would he want to put himself in the way of danger again?

Once bitten, twice shy, was a cliché for all the right reasons.

He wanted to put his feet up, eat good food, enjoy central heating and not have to worry about a fat-fingered man trying to kill him.

But now, in a nice comfortable seat on the SOS jet, somewhere over the Atlantic, Michael didn't feel quite so averse to having another adventure. He knew he was looking at what had happened from the perspective of someone who had survived, and that inevitably meant that he was wearing rose-tinted glasses, but the fact was that he *had* survived, he had taken everything that Mother Nature and evil men could throw at him, and here he was, safe as houses.

Mr Crown, Bonsoir, Dr Faustus and Dr Kincaid were asleep. Bailey, obviously, was flying the jet. Katya was in the seat behind, intently studying her mobile phone. It had been retrieved from the body of the fat-fingered man, or what was left of him after the wolves picked him clean.

'What's so interesting?' Michael asked.

'You.' She turned the screen so that he could see the video she'd taken of him on his arrival at SOS headquarters. He could see his naked bum, back when she'd pretended to be a nurse. Katya smiled up at him. 'Hard to believe it was only a few days ago.'

'Well, we're both heroes now. Maybe you should delete it.'

'Mr Crown says that as soon as you start thinking you're a hero, you inevitably end up injured or dead. I think I'll keep this, just so that I can remind you what an idiot you are.'

Michael sighed. 'I'm too tired to fight.'

'Too lazy, more like.'

Michael sat back in his seat. No matter what she said, she couldn't annoy him. He was on too much of a high.

He closed his eyes. Not to sleep. Dr Faustus was right. He should create a mental picture. Even though he had spent the past twelve hours telling and retelling their adventures, first to his SOS colleagues, then to the police, then the reporters, that had been for *them*, this would be one for *him*.

It had been incredible.

Frightening, *harrowing*, *painful* and above all, *freezing*, but yes, definitely, incredible.

And it wasn't over. It might *never* be over.

Even though Dr Kincaid would have preferred to keep the Eden under wraps until they could prove scientifically that it had actually been shot down, they really had no alternative but to display it outside the Miller Hotel once the reporters and cameramen saw it on their sledge. Within seconds pictures of their discovery were on the internet, and very quickly after that on news channels and newspapers. They were famous.

But far from answering questions, their discovery of the Eden just prompted more, which inevitably set off a war of words between governments, scientists, conspiracy theorists, religious maniacs, reporters – between every shade of opinion.

What also remained a mystery was the identity of the fake camera crew who had discovered the Eden in the first place. Were they working for themselves? Bounty hunters or treasure seekers? Or were they working for whatever business conglomerate or foreign power had ordered the destruction of the Eden in the first place? What the police were able to tell them was that they had been unable to recover fingerprints from the two bodies. Michael had thought this meant that their hands had been eaten by the bear. But no, it meant that their fingerprints had been chemically burned off at some point in the past to prevent them being identified. It didn't stop them taking DNA samples, of course, but these led nowhere. The fat-fingered man had been expecting to be picked up either by helicopter, snowmobile or sledge. He had failed to make it to their rendezvous point. But who was doing the picking up?

In a quiet moment, Michael had asked Dr Kincaid who he thought really was responsible both for shooting down the Eden, and for the attempt to steal its remains.

'I could tell you,' replied Dr Kincaid, 'but then I'd have to kill you.'

It was an old joke.

Michael said, 'I'm serious. You can tell me.'

Dr Kincaid gave a slight shake of his head. 'Son,' he said, 'it used to be that we knew who all the bad guys were – they wore uniforms and marched up and down waving the flags of their countries. They invaded. They took prisoners. But that's all changed. One man with a laptop can do as much damage as an army of ten thousand men. There are forces out there greater than you can imagine – they defy national boundaries, they don't adhere to any religion. The only thing they seem to have in common is a lust for power and wealth.'

Michael nodded for several long moments. Then he said, 'Yes, but do you know who *this* was?'

'No. Not yet. He, she, they or it might not even have a name. But I know what you're thinking – it's important to give evil a name. Well, if it helps, give it one. Call it . . . Frank. We're SOS, Michael; we're trying to save the world, and Frank is trying to stop us. Everywhere we go, Frank is going to turn up. So keep your eyes peeled.'

Michael kind of liked the idea of Frank.

The good news as far as the Inuit of Miller's Harbour were concerned was that Jordan underwent emergency surgery to have a bullet removed from his chest, and was expected to make a full recovery. His grandfather Paul Nappaaluk, meanwhile, was released from prison and the charges against him dropped after police took statements about the attack of the giant polar bear from Michael and Katya, and examined the different locations where the members of the fake camera crew were killed. Jordan was being hailed as a hero, tourists were already flocking into town, and business looked as if it was about to, almost literally, rocket.

They had managed to visit Jordan briefly in the hospital before leaving. He was all covered in wires and tubes and bandages, but there was colour back in his cheeks, and a wonderful lightness in his eyes. He said, 'Sorry about running off like that, but I had to . . .'

'We weren't letting you go,' said Katya.

'Were they terrible to you?' asked Michael. 'The bad guys?'

'Well, they shot me, I guess that is pretty terrible. They thought I was looking for the satellite as well and put a bullet in me when I wouldn't stop the sledge; truth is I didn't see or hear them till it hit me, I was listening to my music. Then their own GPS froze up and the weather closed in, and they thought me being local I'd know how to get them out of there. They weren't to know I knew nothing about finding my way round – I can just about make my way to KFC unaccompanied.'

Katya smiled and took hold of his hand. 'Jordan, we know you're not as dumb as you make out. You were after the bear, and you found it.'

'I think in the end, it found me. To save me. My grandfather, he ain't so dumb either. He knows things.'

Michael opened his eyes again and saw that Dr Kincaid was now awake and studying his laptop. He got up and walked over. Michael cleared his throat. Dr Kincaid glanced up.

'Hi – thought you were sleeping.'

'Can't.'

'Still wired, eh? Have a seat.' Michael sat beside him. Dr Kincaid studied him for several moments. 'What's eating you now?'

'Nothing.'

'Something is.'

'Well. I was just thinking about SOS. What worries me is that we're supposed to be saving things, but now it's all over the internet and the news channels about this giant man-eating bear, and that means the place is going to be swarming with even more hunters, and they're going to kill it, and doesn't that defeat the purpose of what SOS is for?'

Dr Kincaid clasped his hands and nodded thoughtfully.

'You're partly right. We are about saving things. But son, what you learn in this business, is you can't save everything. You make choices. Not everything is black and white. Nature is scary. And yes, the bear will be hunted down one way or another. As it happens the police in Miller's Harbour have just emailed me an analysis of the DNA they picked up at the camp ground and from the bodies of the deceased. Ran it through the research centre on the edge of town. Seems the bear's what they call an *ursid hybrid* – result of a polar bear and a grizzly bear getting together.'

'Is that even possible?'

'It's very rare, I'll give you that, but not unknown. They're genetically similar. And this is where we come in, and the Eden. You see, grizzly or brown bears live and breed on land, while polar bears live and breed on the ice. But global warming is causing the ice to thin, which means the polar bears are finding it impossible to hunt there, which is forcing them inland, and so they're bumping into their near relatives more often. And when you get a huge big polar mating with a huge big grizzly, they're going to have huge big kids.'

'It's funny – that bear, it was the most horrific, scary thing I've ever seen. I mean, it tore those guys to pieces . . . but part of me doesn't want to see it killed. It was so . . . impressive.'

Dr Kincaid smiled. 'I'm sure he was. And I'm sure he's still out there somewhere. He has thousands of miles to roam across. I understood there was a GPS system that was monitoring him, but it seems to have been mysteriously smashed.'

Michael looked guiltily away. 'I think Katya dropped it.'

Dr Kincaid was fixing him with a look.

'Or it may have been me.'

'Well, accidents happen. It improves his chances, at any rate. Maybe some hunters will get him. Maybe the authorities will track him down and tranquillize him and study him; see if he's a one-off or maybe the start of something new. Thing is, Michael, we think we know everything about this planet, but we don't know the half of it, not even a third or an eighth. Constantly surprising you. It's what keeps me at it.'

Above them, Bailey's voice came out of a small speaker, crystal clear: 'Dr Kincaid to the flight deck, please.'

Dr Kincaid rolled his eyes. 'Probably gotten us lost again. If we have to bail out, he's absolutely getting the sack this time.'

He was joking of course.

At least Michael hoped he was joking.

As Dr Kincaid slipped through the cabin door, Michael returned to his own chair and settled back. This time he did begin to drift away. He was back on the snow with the bear, but there was no sense of danger. It was padding slowly away, and Jordan's song, his lament, was the only sound. Michael wondered if Jordan had known how it would affect the bear, if he had deliberately drawn upon thousands of years of Inuit folklore or ancient connection to the wildlife in the Arctic, or if he had just dredged it out of his delirious mind. It might not have influenced the bear at all. Perhaps, having so recently devoured one human, he wasn't hungry and saw no threat in Michael or Katya or Jordan.

Michael was jolted suddenly awake as the jet banked sharply.

All around him the other Artists were already awake.

There was palpable tension in the air.

Michael turned in his seat.

'What . . . what is it?' he asked Katya. 'Has Bailey . . . ?'

'Change of plan.' Her laptop was already open. 'We're on our way to Indonesia.'

'Indonesia? *Why?*'

'Absolutely no idea.'

But her eyes were alive with excitement.

Just like his own.

Mount Taron, Indonesia.
Michael and Katya are racing towards a volcano, but it's about to blow. The earthquakes are getting more and more dangerous, the river is boiling, and the SOS team is out of reach.

Michael and Katya have to carry out a rescue alone, against all the odds. But are they being lured into a trap?

ISBN 978-0-340-99887-8